BOOKS BY QUINN AVERY
www.QuinnAvery.com

BEXLEY SQUIRES MYSTERY SERIES

The Dead Girl's Stilettos

The Million Dollar Collar

The Guard's Last Watch

The Skeleton Key's Secrets

The Notebook's Hidden Truths

The Neighbor's Dark Past

STANDALONE ROMANTIC SUSPENSE/THRILLERS

What They Never Said

In Her Father's Shadow

Woman Over the Edge

Deadly Paradise

Lost Girls of Kato

Moscow Mules & Murder

Right Across the Bay

CHILDREN'S BOOKS WRITTEN BY QUINN

Dogs Don't Have Fins

Dogs Don't Have Antlers

The Dead Girl's Stilettos
The Million Dollar Collar
The Guard's Last Watch
The Skeleton Key's Secrets
The Notebook's Hidden Truths
The Neighbor's Dark Past

THE MILLION DOLLAR COLLAR

A BEXLEY SQUIRES MYSTERY

QUINN AVERY

The Million Dollar Collar: A Bexley Squires Mystery

Cover Design: Najla Qamber

Model: Samantha Naumann

Photography © 2019 Jennifer Naumann

ISBN: 9781086373936

PROLOGUE

PAPAYA SPRINGS, CALIFORNIA

AUGUST 24TH

Heidi Steele flicked a crushed smoke into the dumpster behind La Belle, swearing under her breath. Her budget didn't allow for more vape juice, and the rawness of the carcinogens in her boyfriend's menthol cigarette ripped through her lungs like a hacksaw. All too often she dreamed what it must be like to have the kind of dough her patrons flaunted. Papaya Springs was overloaded with entitled trust-fund babies who couldn't tolerate beads of sweat on their glasses, nor would they stand to have their Carbonara served a mere degree colder than expected. The number of college kids flashing their daddies' money had outnumbered the older crowd, and they were ten times worse than their parents.

Heidi would give anything to not give a damn how much diapers or formula cost, not to mention her baby girl's medical bills that loomed over her like a formidable mountain. Hell, she'd volunteer her right arm in the name of science if it meant she'd never have to worry about procuring rent money ever again.

Her favorite coworker slipped through the employee entrance into the alley, eyebrows shooting up to his respectably thick hairline. "What's happenin', hot stuff?"

She let out a tinkling giggle, knowing he was merely trying to cheer her up with a quote from her favorite movie. "Oh, just the usual…trying to pretend my life doesn't royally suck in comparison to those jerk-wards inside."

If she wasn't committed to Davis because they'd made a child together, she'd consider giving Travis one of the dates he was always offering. Those deep dimples and bright green eyes of his got her motor running. Plus he drove a classic Mustang and rented a decent house in Fullerton, so he didn't seem to be short on cash like her deadbeat baby daddy.

Waitressing for the affluent community was her

only source of income, yet she felt a deep contention toward it that she couldn't put into words. After serving the residents of Papaya Springs for over five years, she was seriously starting to despise the entire human race. She motioned to the restaurant, eyes rolling to the dark sky. "Still crazy in there?"

Travis lifted a broad shoulder. He worked out regularly, and rocked the white button-down and black slacks required of every chef at La Belle. But the way the moonlight reflected in his dazzling eyes made Heidi's stomach flutter. Maybe he'd be up for a little messing around.

"No different from any other Saturday night." He pulled a vape pen from his pocket and took a drag before eyeing her, hesitant. "Want some?"

The rich vanilla scent brought a smile to her lips. "Yes please."

Smoke billowed from his nose as he handed it over. She was all at once happy as she inhaled the smooth flavor and her limbs grew heavy. Travis, a small-time dealer, was known for lacing his vape with weed, and it was exactly what she needed to ease the tension of waiting on ten tables in the span of one hour. Head tilted back, she returned the pen to him and sighed. "Two more hours before I'm outta here. If I hear one more request tonight for gluten free bread or something vegan, I'm torching the place to the ground."

Lips quirked with a grin, Travis titled his head. "You plannin' to go anywhere after? I heard a table full of PSC kids talking about a sick party one of the sororities is throwing down on the beach later." He took another hit and grinned. "Figure we could crash it—give them a taste of how the other half likes to party."

Heidi bit her bottom lip. Last time he made that kind of offer, he gave her a decent cut of his earnings for the night after she'd sent a group of college girls his way. Her mom was watching the baby until she got off work, but Davis would be done less than an hour later, and they needed the extra money. "I'll go, but only if you give me thirty percent this time."

Their conversation was interrupted by the sound of several girls giggling nearby, followed by the squeal of tires. Heidi rolled her eyes, wondering what it must be like to come from a rich family and have endless free time to mess around.

A moment later, Travis pointed at something behind Heidi. "Bruh…what the hell is that?"

Heidi turned, expecting practically anything

other than the puffy white dog that emerged from the shadows. Splatters of dried mud covered the otherwise beautiful animal's matted fur, and its ears were tight against its head like it had been spooked. As it trotted toward the two coworkers, its bubble-gum pink tongue and curly tail both began to wag.

"Hey there, pretty girl." Heidi held out her hand to the dog, palm upward. "You lost?"

"No collar," Travis commented. "Probably a stray. Wouldn't touch that raggedy thing if I were you…probably isn't up to date on shots."

She let the dog lick her hand anyway. The warm, tough tongue seemed exceptionally dry. "He's friendly enough. Poor thing probably ran away from its owners while chasing something."

Travis bent down to the dogs level, squinting. "*Dude*. He kinda looks like the dog that was on the news yesterday—the one some famous lady lost. You know who I'm talking about…on that show where she's always buying stupid shit, and going on fancy trips around the world. The hot Spanish lady that's into fairytales."

"You mean Temperance Rose?" Heidi's pulse kicked up a notch as she watched the dog continue to lick her hand. Her vision filled with dollar signs. Rumor had it, the reality star had paid a cool million for the rare breed. Could she be so lucky? "Oh my god, you're right! It kind of *does* look like her dog!"

The dog leapt over to Travis, dirtying his knees. He cursed and stood upright, brushing his pant legs. "Stupid mutt. Let's tie it up. You can take it home when you get off for the night, and we'll try to sell it on Craigslist or some shit."

"I can't have pets in my apartment." She suddenly felt protective of the dog as it cuddled in against her legs, wagging its butt when she scratched behind his ear. And anyway, she loved Temperance Rose—she seemed so sweet on her show. Plus there was a chance Heidi could make just as much—maybe even *more*—if Temperance was offering any kind of reward. "If we tried to sell it, the cops might find out and accuse us of stealing him in the first place."

"Whatever." Travis slipped the vape pen back into his pocket and shrugged. "If you decide you want to crash that party, come meet me at closing." Whistling an old 80s rock ballad, he strolled back inside.

Heidi cooed when the dog rolled around to its back, waiting for her to scratch his tummy. She humored her, laughing. "Who's a good girl? You're gonna make me rich!"

A moment later, Jessica, one of their coworkers peered out the restaurant's back door and frowned at the dog. "Where did that mutt come from?"

"It's mine," Heidi lied. "She ran away a couple nights ago…must've remembered where I work."

"Well your break was over five minutes ago. Get your ass back inside."

Heidi nodded. "I'm just going to tie her up back here until my shift's over, then I'll be right in."

She smiled as she continued to scratch the dog's tummy, envisioning all the ways her life was about to change.

PART I

CHAPTER ONE

PAPAYA SPRINGS, CALIFORNIA

AUGUST 26TH

The main line of Stronghold Investigations rang in a shrill sound that irritated Bexley Squires's already throbbing headache. She'd been putting in late hours for seven straight days, hoping to catch one of the city's most influential CEOs in the act of fornicating with one of his many mistresses. His wife of ten years and two months was offering to pay Bexley top dollar for physical proof of his affairs so she could collect on his benefits. Since Bexley hadn't succeeded in getting the money shot, it made her question yet again if she had the skill set or *cojones* to become a licensed private investigator.

"You gonna get that?" J.J.'s deep voice drawled from the hallway.

Thinking her boss had left hours ago, Bexley let out a yelp before grabbing the ancient rotary phone from its cradle. Since nearly falling prey to Papaya Springs' resident serial killer at the beginning of the year, she was still jittery. She slept with her bedroom light on, and her newly licensed handgun tucked beneath her mattress. There were a few times she had scared the living hell out of her sister, thinking Cineste was an intruder.

"Stronghold Investigations," she choked out.

"Bex?" Grayson's deep voice boomed through the earpiece. "Everything alright? I thought you were coming over for dinner with my parents. Why aren't you answering your cell?"

Bexley silently mouthed a line of curse words to the popcorn ceiling. It seemed a lifetime ago that her hot detective boyfriend had invited her over to finally sample his famous prime rib. Her mouth watered as she envisioned it on her plate, oozing with juice.

But she hadn't seen his parents since high school, and she was in no hurry to revisit a torturous session with Ben and Kitty Rivers, two of Papaya Springs' most influential socialites.

She fumbled with the phone as she tried to hold it between her cheek and shoulder. "Yeah…ah…I still am. Just finishing up here, and I'll be on my way."

"You've been clocking more time there than I've spent with the FBI," he grumbled in a tone thick with irritation. "Thought you agreed to take some time off."

The idea of prime rib vanished. *Not this again.* "There was no such agreement made. That was simply *you* telling *me* to cut back because you aren't happy with our arrangement. Just because I'm a woman doesn't make me a porcelain doll, Grayson. I *can* work just as hard as you without breaking."

His voice softened. "Never said you can't. I'm just pissed off that I never get to spend any time with my girl."

Her heart sank a little. Things had been chaotic from the moment she'd begun the move back to Papaya Springs from New York. She couldn't remember the last time she'd spent the night at Grayson's. It had been a grueling summer as she logged in excessive hours to apply toward her private investigator's license. She missed the easy-going mannerisms of their relationship when they were first reunited. When they were constantly throwing playful jabs at each other. When they were insatiable in the sack.

Phone held close to her lips, she thought of the prime rib once again. "You could make sure my wine glass is always full to guarantee I'll spend the night. Cineste is having company over anyway."

A noise of discontent rumbled against Grayson's throat. "Is she still spending time with Commander Peachtree's son?"

Bexley sighed heavily while rubbing at one of her temples. She knew Grayson would never approve of her sister's complicated relationship with Alex. Bexley wasn't sure she understood it either. Last fall, Cineste had decided to run off with the former Navy SEAL just minutes before she'd been drugged and kidnapped. It bothered Bexley to no end that Alex shared the same blood as the man who'd forced Cineste into prostitution. The Commander had organized the ill-fated boys' club. And it was because of him that those women became Dean Halliwell's prey.

Bexley and Grayson had each played an active role in bringing down the former Hollywood actor and the boys' club that had covered up his string of murders. Then in early spring, Grayson had part-nered up with a team of special agents to track down more missing women nationwide who may have also been the actor's victims.

"I'll take your silence as a confirmation," Grayson said. "When's she gonna realize that guy's a loose cannon?"

"Probably around the same time society realizes it's impossible to find a soulmate by swiping right."

"Damn it, Bex. We'd see each other a helluva lot more if you'd stop being so stubborn. When are you going to finally agree to move in with me like I've been pleading for months?"

There wasn't a witty comeback to that question. The idea of becoming domesticated was as appealing as a full lobotomy. How would he react when he discovered she was a terrible cook, or that she let her laundry go until she'd worn every last pair of underwear on both sides? Cineste barely tolerated her antics, and she was just as messy. Grayson liked things orderly, and kept his place spotless. Shacking up together would open a whole new realm of awkwardness in their relationship.

There was a long pause before he cleared his throat. "Like I keep saying, if it's because of my neighborhood, we could always search for a place right on the beach. I know how much you like being close to the ocean. We could easily afford it with our combined salaries."

Bexley's teeth chomped together. Sharing a dwelling was an even bigger leap than she was willing to take. What would he want next? Tramp stamps bearing each other's names? Vials of each other's blood worn around their necks? Dare she say it—*marriage?* "I don't think Cineste is ready to live on her own."

"Why not? She's attending NA on a regular basis, and meeting with her counselor twice a week. Her job's going well, and she's spending time with her old friends. She has a good handle on her sobriety. Sounds to me like you're fishing for an excuse."

He wasn't totally wrong. "That may be so, but she still isn't sleeping much. And when she finally passes out, she wakes from night terrors. I don't want to push her if she isn't ready to live on her own."

"Then maybe we should look into a two-bedroom. Wouldn't hurt to keep an eye on her as long as she's still hanging around that guy."

A long sigh fell from Bexley's nose. It didn't seem there was any way to talk him out of the idea, and she wasn't ready to disclose that she was still struggling just as much as her sister. Having

Grayson's protection would be a game-changer, but she wasn't willing to accept that she needed to lean on anyone. "She's finally getting comfortable having her own place. I doubt she'd want to become our houseguest."

"Is there another reason you're fighting me on this? Are you having second thoughts about being with me?"

"What? No!"

"Don't jerk me around, Bex." His voice was all at once soft and pleading. "This thing with you—it's the real deal. It makes what I had with Amanda seem like a bad joke. This is it for me. If you want out, I'd rather find out now than later on down the road when I'm ready to take the next step."

The next step? The temptation to bang her head on the desk was strong. Was it really necessary to have that conversation in that very moment, *over the phone?* Why did she have to fall for a guy who always insisted on hashing his feelings to death? He was constantly asking her if she loved him, or if she was even capable of love. Until they met, she hadn't been aware one stupid word could have so much power.

"Grayson, I'm—"

There was a heavy knock on her office door

before J.J. pushed his way inside. The old PI appeared primed for a hot date—fluffy white hair slicked back, silver hoop earring rather than the usual diamond stud, sports jacket thrown over a Pink Floyd T-shirt. Then again, it was similar to what he had worn to both his oldest buddy's funeral, and his neighbor kid's wedding, so he could virtually be headed anywhere. He was the kind of laid back, understanding man Bexley wished her military-minded father could've been. She'd grown quite fond of her new mentor, and his straight-shooting ways.

"Someone's here to see you, darlin'." His eyes widened considerably, but his deep voice remained steady. In the handful of months they'd been working together, they'd learned to read each other's body language, and she knew he was warning her to prepare herself. "Says she's an old friend of yours."

He nudged the door open the rest of the way, allowing Temperance Rose to step in around him. The sultry reality star wore black leggings and a plain tank top that were as much out of character as the careless way she'd pulled her dark hair back tight against her head in a disheveled ponytail, and the natural glow of her makeup-free cheeks. There wasn't any sign of the graceful, carefree woman who had once graciously welcomed Bexley into her home. She met Bexley's dumfounded gaze with flitting eyes and a timid smile.

"Grayson, I gotta run," Bexley said into the phone. His gruff response was cut short when she set the phone back on its cradle. She folded her hands over the desk and matched the woman's smile. "Temperance. This is certainly a surprise."

J.J. paused a moment, watching Bexley thoughtfully, waiting for any sign that she didn't want to be left alone. "I'll let you two have at it." Bexley answered him with a dip of her chin, and J.J. exited, closing the door behind him.

Bexley took a steadying breath. The last time she'd seen Temperance was when she'd taken the stand at Dean Halliwell's murder trial. Hearing the movie star's ex-girlfriend speak of their relationship in front of the jury had dredged up a whirlwind of unpleasant memories. Not because of anything Temperance had done, of course, but because it reminded Bexley of the way she'd briefly felt when Dean had played on her weaknesses. She'd let him kiss her, and he turned out to be a serial killer. It saddened her to think of how it must've crushed Temperance once she discovered the man she once wanted to marry was capable of killing innocent women with his bare hands.

"Sorry to visit you at such a late hour." Temperance's heavy accent wavered with every word, as if she was close to breaking into tears. "I would've waited until morning if I didn't desperately need your help."

Bexley nodded and stood, offering a kind smile. "It's no problem. Please, have a seat."

The women lowered across from each other at the same time. An apology lodged in Bexley's throat. After Dean's arrest, it was all over the news that Temperance's reality show had been cancelled indefinitely. Did Temperance blame Bexley for ruining her life?

"How have you been holding up?" Bexley's voice was soft, filled with empathy. Part of her wanted to reach over the table and embrace the woman. The fun spark of energy Temperance had the day they met was long gone.

"What happened still hurts…and makes me sad." Temperance's lips trembled with a little smile that didn't reach her eyes. "But every day…it gets a little better." She squirmed in her seat. hands folded. "In court, you mentioned you worked here now. I need your help with something *importante*. My dog, my sweet *Cenicienta*, she was missing for two whole days."

Bexley vividly recalled reading an article that claimed Temperance had paid a million dollars for the rare Samoyed breed. Losing her beloved pet was the last thing the poor woman deserved, but it seemed life had a habit of kicking a person when they're down. "You said *was*. Does that mean you've found her?" she asked with a surge of hope.

Temperance flashed a wide smile. "*Sí*. A waitress from La Belle contacted my social media manager, said she came to her in an alley behind her restaurant. She thought it was Cinderella because she'd seen her mentioned in the news. Poor love was dirty and so very happy to see her *mamá*." Then her gaze was once again haunted with grief. "Only her collar—one that was custom made in Paris—was missing."

Bexley remembered how the dog's collar had sparkled with what she suspected were diamonds when she met the white ball of fur. "Do you think the woman might've kept it?"

"She swears no—says she came to her without it."

"Did you file a report with the police?"

"Only that Cinderella had gone missing. My

assistant let them know when she had returned, but I didn't want her to mention the collar."

Bexley's eyes widened. "Why not?"

"I've made too many headlines already. I don't want the details of the collar to become public. It's quite valuable—worth over a million dollars. But that's not why it's *especial*." Tears pooled in Temperance's big brown eyes, and her lips began to tremble. "It was the last thing he ever gave me."

With a flicker of understanding, Bexley handed Temperance the tissue box from the corner of her desk. "It was a gift from Dean."

"*Sí*. He said he wanted to give me a reason to smile after he was gone." Temperance took a tissue and gingerly dabbed at her eyes. Then, setting a hand on the desk between them, she met Bexley's gaze. "I knew you of all people would understand. You must've believed he was good when you agreed to clear his name." Fresh tears spilled down her cheeks. "How can someone so sweet be the same monster who killed those poor women?"

Bexley's heart ached as she covered Temperance's hand with her own. "The psychiatrist for the state testified that Dean displays all the traits of a psychopath. There's no way you...me...or anyone else will ever understand how he could do those things." It was solid advice, considering she was repeating some of the things her own therapist had told her during their intense sessions. "He was charming, but he was also incredibly sick. He had everyone in Hollywood convinced he was one of the good guys. And you're not the only one who wanted to believe he was innocent. Stop beating yourself up, trying to get inside his head."

Temperance took another tissue to wipe at her face. *"Gracias."* Then she flipped her free hand around to squeeze Bexley's while holding her stare. "Will you help me, Miss Bexley...*por favor?"*

Even though the long hours she'd put in might cause yet another rift with Grayson, Bexley looked into the kind woman's eyes and knew she couldn't turn her down.

BY THE TIME Bexley wrapped up the interview with Temperance, she sensed she had crossed a line with Grayson long before she found him sulking in his backyard, alone. He stared off into the dark sky, sipping on a glass of what was undoubtedly his favorite whiskey. She kicked herself for not taking the time to message him earlier.

"I'm sorry. A client came in—"

"Save it. I don't want to hear your excuses. My parents stayed as long as they could, but my mom has an early morning appointment." His masculine features were rigid, and the whites of his eyes felt menacing beneath the waning moonlight. Shirt unbuttoned and rolled to his elbows, howling wolf tattoo on his arm on full display, dark hair disheveled from what must've been a trying day, he still took her breath away after all this time. "Your dinner's in the fridge."

Either Bexley was experiencing a serious case of arrhythmia, or it physically pained her knowing she had let him down enough that he couldn't even greet her with a smile. She burst forward, crouching down at his side and grasping his arm. "Please don't do that thing where you shoot me poisonous glares all night, and treat me like I'm your biggest disappointment. I fulfilled my tolerance for that shit with my father years ago."

The tension between his beautiful eyes lifted. "Damn it, Bex, What do you want me to say? We don't seem to have the same end game in mind."

"Are you kidding me? I have my eye on the goalie guy too. We both know I have emotional range of a rock on a good day, but I've never wanted anything as badly as I want this relationship to last. We'll just have to keep working on the other stuff…figure out what makes us happy." She tugged one of his hands away from his glass, and threaded their fingers together. "I'm disgustingly and unforgivingly late because Temperance Rose came to ask for my help. You know what she's been through…I couldn't just send her away."

Bexley could literally see his anger evaporating when he pulled her up to sit in his lap. "I heard something mentioned at the station the other day about her dog." Everything felt right again as he hooked her around the waist, flashing the kind of concerned look that had made her fall so hard for him back in high school. "Is she alright?"

"Not really. She still seems pretty messed up." She looped her arm around his head, and fingered his recently cut hair. "Off the record—just between you and me? She got her dog back, but it was missing an outrageously expensive collar with sentimental value. She came to me because she doesn't want the public to know the specifics."

"Guess this means you'll be putting in even more hours." Grayson released a long, resolved breath. "Will you at least talk with J.J. to see if he'll lighten your load? Maybe I could even help you out with some of the leg work." A flirty smile curled his lips as he traced his fingers along her thigh. "We both know how much I like making these legs work."

"See, now this, *this* is exactly one of the reasons why I keep you around." She bent down to brush her lips over his, letting them linger for a delayed second before pulling back. "You know better than to try to talk me out of something, even if you don't agree with what I'm doing. And I'm sorry about your parents…I really am. We'll reschedule as soon as things aren't so crazy."

Grayson gathered her in his strong arms, surrounding her with his earthly scent. The scent of *home*.

"You drive me insane, but it's a big part of the reason I like having *you* around," he whispered. "Let's continue this inside."

CHAPTER TWO

A psychedelic orange glow breached the horizon as Bexley rang the doorbell of Heidi Steele's apartment in Eastside Santa Ana. The neighborhood was infamous due to a recent influx of gang violence, and drive-bys. With every sideways glance she'd received on her way from the parking lot to the third floor, she'd touched her fingertips to her leather handbag. The Glock she'd picked out with Grayson was always within reach. She had a standing date Tuesday nights at the shooting range with Cineste, sometimes taking Grayson along to provide them with pointers. The sisters had both become excellent marksmen. Still, Bexley had reservations about sticking a bullet inside another human.

After a shouted, *"Calm your tits, I'm coming!"* and some fumbling noises from inside, the paint-chipped door finally swung open. A tall, lanky brunette in a wrinkled T-shirt and no pants cradled a sleeping infant in one arm, eyeing Bexley with disdain. She hardly looked old enough to drive, but Bexley didn't have room for that kind of judgment.

Bexley flashed a kind, bright smile. "Are you Heidi Steele?"

The woman slammed the door shut in Bexley's face. "I was told there wouldn't be any more well-being checks!" she yelled.

Pounding on the door, Bexley shouted, "I'm actually here to see if you can answer a few questions about the dog you found!"

After a beat, the door slowly creaked back open. The young woman's eyes narrowed with suspicion. "Why? I already returned it."

Bexley held up a professional 8x10 Temperance had taken of her dog on its last birthday, perched on a pillar and wearing a crown. The backdrop of hundreds of balloons, glitter, streamers, and garish floral arrangements was ten times more elaborate than any celebration Bexley had attended for a human. "I'm trying to track down the whereabouts of this collar."

She carefully gaged the young woman's reaction as she spoke, sensing complete surprise. Or maybe it was simply the same kind of astonishment Bexley felt when she first witnessed the absurdity of the animal's pampering.

"Those real diamonds?" Heidi asked in a hushed voice.

"Do you know where it might be?"

"You think I'd still be living in this shithole if I did?" The little pink bundle in the woman's arms began to squirm. She grunted with irritation. "If that's all—"

"Were you alone when you found her dog?"

The young woman's eyes darted to the left, and her voice jumped an octave when she said, "Yeah… of course. It was Saturday, so it was too busy for more than one of us to break at the same time."

"Do you remember anything unusual that happened while you were the alley, *before* the dog appeared? Maybe a voice, or a vehicle that didn't belong in the neighborhood?"

"Now that you mention it, I heard a bunch of girls laughing," Heidi said, nodding. "And tires squealing." Chewing on her lip, she started to shut the door in Bexley's face. "But that's all I know. Now if you don't mind—"

Bexley leaned her shoulder into the door, preventing it from closing any farther. The woman was displaying all the classic tells involved with a lie. Shifty eyes. A need to be done. "Actually, would it be alright if I used your bathroom?"

Heidi set a hand on her hip. "You aren't serious."

"Not always, but I drank like a gallon of water this morning, and my other option is that convenience store around the corner with bars on the windows and gang symbols spray-painted on the door."

Heidi's shoulders relaxed. "I wouldn't want to go there either. I heard someone once got crabs from their toilet seats." She gave Bexley one final sweep with her eyes before pulling the door back open. "Knock yourself out. Down the hallway to the left."

The woman's fear of a well-being check was immediately transparent. The stench of stale cigarettes and rotten food roiled Bexley's stomach. The place clearly hadn't been tidied up in weeks, maybe even months. Piles of clothes and dirty dishes were the apartment's predominant decor. With dark pile carpet throughout, it should've been easy to determine whether or not a Samoyed dog had spent any amount of time there in recent days. According to Temperance, her dog shed its weight in white hairs, leaving proof of its existence in every nook and cranny of her house.

As the mother tried to comfort her fussy baby, Bexley took her time strolling through the place, eagerly scanning the floor and ratty furniture for signs Temperance's beloved Cinderella had dropped a proverbial shoe.

By the time she found her way to the bathroom, she'd already decided there was no way she was going to use the woman's urine-stained toilet. She ran the sink for a good minute, turning it off when she heard the escalated voice of a man from the other room. For what must've been the tenth time that morning, her fingers brushed over the cool metal of the handgun inside her handbag. She extracted her stun gun instead, and cracked the door open. She certainly wasn't going to wield a deadly weapon with a newborn in the mix.

"Where's the money?" a deep, gravelly voice shouted.

"I told you already!" Heidi cried. "I put it toward Casey's hospital bills! I swear!"

Bexley darted around the corner to find a man in his twenties with long, greasy hair as black as coal wearing a wife-beater stained with oil. He loomed over Heidi, gripping one of her arms as the baby wailed in the other. Their gazes fell on Bexley at the same time. The man's burned with contempt. Heidi's filled with relief.

His lip curled upward. "Who are you?"

"She's a friend—from work," Heidi lied, casting Bexley a pleading look. "She wanted to know if I could cover for her tonight."

Bexley found it interesting that Heidi didn't want the man knowing the real reason Bexley had paid her a visit. Did that mean she *did* know the whereabouts of the collar?

The man pointed at Bexley's stun gun. "What the hell's that for?"

"It's a precaution in case I run into any angry assholes threatening women holding small children." She eyed Heidi. The woman's lips were white with tension. "Are you okay?"

Heidi nodded, eyes darting to the left. "This is my boyfriend, Davis…Casey's father."

"Well, *Davis*," Bexley addressed the man sharply, "what's it going to be? A jolt to the nuts and a call to child services, or a short break from your family until you can get your anger under control?"

She depressed the stun gun, letting the crackling noise be his last warning.

The man released Heidi, eyeing Bexley with hostility. "Someone should teach you to mind your own business."

"And someone should teach *you* the repercussions of domestic assault," she retorted, heading for the doorway. She held it open, motioning for him to exit. "Have a lovely day, *Davis*."

He held her gaze for a chilling moment before he sulked out the door. He turned to spit onto the doorstep before the door swung shut behind him.

Heidi moaned. "You shouldn't have done that."

"He seems dangerous. Do you really want to raise your daughter in that kind of environment?" Bexley slipped her a business card. "Call me if you remember anything else about the night you found Ms. Rose's dog." She held her stare for a beat longer. "If you need help filing a restraining order, I'd be willing to help with that, free of charge."

Heidi let the door close between them without further comment. Bexley kept her fingers coiled around the handgun in her handbag all the way back to her car.

LA BELLE WAS a swanky Italian restaurant in the heart of downtown Papaya Springs—an area Bexley preferred to avoid at all costs. By now the pompous residents recognized her, and saw her as a threat. And whenever she was with Grayson, she could count on being approached over petty cases that weren't worth his time. They were better off slumming it over greasy burgers in another part of town.

Bexley shuddered the moment she entered the establishment. They had yet to open for the lunch crowd, but even when empty it still somehow omitted an ostentatious vibe between the pristine tablecloths and dark wood accents dimly lit by modern pendants. The heavenly aroma of baked lasagna reminded Bexley that she had turned down Grayson's offer for breakfast in bed.

An older hostess in an impeccably pressed uniform rushed toward Bexley, her graying hair twisted into a bun behind her narrow head, bright lipstick fresh on her thin lips. "We don't open for another twenty-one minutes," she snapped.

Bexley bit her tongue with the need to correct the woman as the digital clock behind her had ticked down another minute. Messing with her type was one of Bexley's favorite past-times, but she tried her best to behave now that she answered to J.J.

"Oh, I'm not here to eat," Bexley said. "I was here on Saturday night, and wondered if I could have a moment with your wait staff."

The woman's eyes widened in surprise. "Did you have a problem with your meal?"

"No, it's nothing like that. I lost a valuable necklace—a family heirloom—and there was a message on my phone from one of your staff saying they'd found it." She wanted to catch the staff off-guard before she had a chance to meet with them as first reactions tended to be revealing. "My husband already retrieved it, but I wanted to thank this Good Samaritan in person."

"Our staff exudes class—I wouldn't expect anything less." The hostess flashed Bexley a stiff smile. "I'll check the schedule to see if anyone from that night is here today."

A handful of moments later, the woman returned with a rigid expression. "Travis, one of our chefs, is out back on break. He's the only one here who was on Saturday. Perhaps he knows which of our staff members assisted you." Her lips pinched together as she waited for Bexley's reaction.

Bexley flashed a waning smile. Was she

expecting a curtsey? "Okay, then. Thank you for your help." She promptly headed back outside, well aware that the woman was watching her every move. Would she ever be able to converse with Papaya Springs residents without wondering if there was a scarlet letter embroidered on her chest?

Behind the restaurant, a young man in a white button-down and black slacks sucked on a vape pen, giving Bexley a thorough once-over. His eyebrows quirked over extremely bloodshot eyes that settled on her breasts. Bexley held in a snort. *Real classy staff, lady.*

"You the one lookin' for someone who was working Saturday night?"

Bexley slid her hands into her back pockets. "Depends on whether or not you're that someone."

He smiled, popping two deep dimples into his cheeks. "I'm your man, sweetheart."

"Not your sweetheart," Bexley protested in a dry, yet friendly tone. She retrieved the picture of Cinderella from her bag. "I'm hoping you can tell me something about this dog."

Travis took the picture and studied it carefully. "I was in this same spot when one kind of like it came wandering around on Saturday. Can't be sure it was the same mutt though. The one I saw was dirty, and he sure as hell wasn't wearing that fancy collar. One of the waitresses talked about selling it on Craigslist. I didn't want anything to do with that shit." He handed the picture back to Bexley, frowning. "Bruh, was it really that rich chick's dog?"

"If by 'rich chick' you mean Temperance Rose, then yeah, *bruh*, it's her dog. And the dog was returned, but the *fancy collar* has sentimental value, and it's missing." Her eyes yearned to roll upward. "What direction did the dog come from?"

He shrugged one shoulder, gesturing to his right. "That way, I guess."

"Anything unusual about its appearance or behavior stand out to you?"

"Yeah. After my shift, I noticed red and silver glitter on my pants. Either that canine was moonlighting as a stripper, or it came from one helluva party."

Was this guy for real? She handed him one of her cards. "If you can think of anything else that might be helpful, please give me a call."

He glanced down at her info, one eyebrow cocked. "How about I use this number to ask you out instead? We could smoke some premium weed together under the stars, and—"

She patted his shoulder, perhaps harder than she should have. "Stay classy, Travis."

EN ROUTE to meeting Grayson for dinner, Bexley decided to change into something more casual than the slacks and trendy leather jacket she wore when on the clock. The parking lot facing the townhouse she shared with Cineste was predictably quiet. The smaller complex on the south edge of town was occupied by middle class millennials who either attended community college during the day and worked until late hours of the night, or worked themselves to the bone during the daytime and otherwise kept to themselves. Rent for the clean two-bedroom was affordable, and their landlord was a pleasant widow who wore too much rouge, and shamelessly hit on any man with a pulse.

Bexley started for their unit's designated stall only to discover it was already occupied by Alex's rusted-out Jeep. She parked behind it, quietly cursing Cineste for her houseguest's behavior. Hopping out of her newly acquired Ford Expedition—a purchase she'd been pressured into by Grayson because of its safety features—she pushed the fob lock. Tingles shot down her spine and radiated over her scalp. The premonition came just seconds before a loud crack whizzed past her right ear. She didn't understand what was happening until there was a similar noise, followed by a metallic ting against the Expedition's door.

Someone was shooting at her. And her gun remained in her handbag on the passenger's seat.

She dropped down to her stomach on the pavement, shimmying around the front of her SUV until she was pressed up against the other side. More shots were fired. The sounds were similar to that of her handgun, which meant they would eventually have to reload. But she didn't have the foresight to keep track of how many bullets there had been so far.

Her heart galloped in her chest. Had Heidi's baby-daddy followed her, wanting to avenge the humiliation she'd bestowed on him? Was Travis that hard up for a date? She'd received a number of threats since bringing down the Commander's Boys' Club. Perhaps her growing fan club was taking their admiration for her to another level, foregoing the "I heart Bexley Squires" apparel.

By dumb luck, she'd stuffed her phone into her back pocket instead of her handbag. She reached back for it, swiping Cineste's number on her home screen.

"Hey!" Her sister's singsong voice alluded that she wasn't alone. "I was just going to call you. We need milk and—"

"Put Alex on the phone," Bexley demanded.

Her sister clicked her tongue. "If this is about him parking—"

"*Now.*" A bullet struck the curb mere inches from her foot. Either someone was a lousy shot, or they were trying to get her attention. They certainly had succeeded with the latter.

"Alright," Cineste mumbled. "Jeez, Bex."

A second later, Alex's deep voice rumbled, "What's up?"

"Someone's trying to put a bullet in me in the condo's parking lot."

"Are you still in your vehicle?" His voice projected intensity.

"No, I'm using it as a shield. By the amount of ammunition they've used so far, I'd say they're pretty determined to get the job done." Another bullet pinged off the vehicle. "Shit!"

"Stay where you are, and don't do anything stupid." He ended the call.

His assumption that she was capable of something "stupid" started a slow, all-consuming burn in the depths of her belly. If she had her gun, she wouldn't have needed to play the damsel card. She hadn't survived Dean Halliwell's attack with stupidity.

Caught up in her anger, the volleying shots fired right behind her came as a complete surprise. She squeaked.

Alex ducked for cover beside her, eyes scanning over the SUV in the distance as he squeezed out another shot. "Are you hurt?"

"Does my pride count?" she gritted through her teeth.

"Did you call nine-one-one?"

"It's a work-related incident. I can handle it on my own."

"Clearly," Alex said as a bullet ricocheted off the pavement and blew out a tire.

When the air became still for several minutes, Bexley let out the breath she'd been holding, and took a minute to steady her heartbeat. She'd been fully aware that dangerous situations would arise once she was working for J.J., but the idea of taking a bullet was terrifying. The blood whooshed from her head when she imagined Cineste and Grayson standing over her casket. She had a lot of life left to live, and was nowhere near ready for it to end.

With a rush of determination, she clambered back to her feet. "I think you scared them off." She turned to face Alex as he rose beside her. "Thanks for your help. Let's keep this incident between us, okay?"

He shook his head slowly, as if disappointed. "Just don't expect me to lie to your boyfriend. I've seen the inside of the local jail cells, and I don't care to go back anytime soon."

CHAPTER THREE

The next morning, Bexley staggered into Stronghold Investigations with a massive energy drink tucked under her arm while trying to bust open a bottle of painkillers. The worst headache of her life was beginning to form. Every noise and flicker of light exaggerated the pounding in her skull. Once she took her SUV in for repairs at her favorite auto body shop just beyond the city limits, she downed a bottle and a half of her favorite Moscato at Grayson's. But it felt necessary to sooth her nerves after the shooting. If the incident had affected her behavior, Grayson didn't seem to notice other than her excessive drinking, so she didn't bring it up. But he had asked why she was driving a loaner vehicle, so she claimed to have gotten into a small fender-bender. She despised herself for lying to him, and swore that she'd tell him the truth if something like that were to happen again.

"Bexley," a deep, familiar voice snapped. "Late as always, I see."

Jerked from her thoughts, Bexley's heart seized as she looked ahead. Decked out in his working uniform, Captain Ferguson stood beside his bride with a protective arm slung behind the beautiful blonde's back. The same sharp green eyes Bexley saw in her mirror filled with tension. A pang spread through her gut as she recalled other times he'd had the same look when she was a child. An angry Captain was a dangerous Captain.

She was beyond shocked to see him for the first time since she'd moved back. How had he known where to find her? And what sane reason would he have to bring her step-mother along?

Both Cineste and Bexley had contested their dad's last marriage to Hillary the prior summer, refusing to attend the oceanside ceremony. The 35-year-old was his second wife following their mother's death, and they simply could not take the busty blonde with any degree of seriousness. Based on the fitting sundress she wore as she stood before her step-daughter, it appeared she'd taken the Trophy Wife look to a new level.

Leona, the elderly receptionist with blue hair who had worked for J.J. since he first went into the business in the mid 80s, leaned across her desk and asked, "Are you alright, Bexley? I have a nice assortment of doughnuts from the bakery down the street."

Bexley flashed the kind woman an appreciative smile. "I'm okay, Leona." Then her gaze swung back to her father and Hillary. "Why are you here?" The greeting lacked warmth or sincerity, the way she'd been brought up by her old man. "What do you want?"

Her father lifted his strong jaw, grinding his teeth. Deep-set wrinkles and gray hairs had aged him considerably, but the gloom behind his stare produced the same unrelenting chill it had given Bexley all her life. "We need your help with a...*delicate* situation." The words were clipped, as if it pained him to ask one of his offspring for their assistance. Frowning, he eyed the paneled hallway. "Do you have an office?"

A smart response involving the broom closet ticked against her tongue, but curiosity got the best of her. Whatever reason he had for breaking their unspoken rift had the potential to be epic. The way Hillary's flawless features remained emotionless, Bexley suspected there was trouble in paradise. She started for the hallway, motioning for them to follow. "Right this way."

She was thankful J.J.'s office door remained closed as they passed. She couldn't handle an exchange between the man who'd raised her, and the man who'd taught her more about being a decent human being in seven months than she'd learned in a lifetime.

Once they entered her pathetically outdated office, she saw every flaw from her father's point of view. In sharp contrast to the other residents of Papaya Springs, J.J. was a simple man who didn't see the point in putting hard-earned money into cosmetics. It showed in the chipped desk and faded leather chair acquired at an estate sale. Bexley was perfectly content with the accommodations until the moment she felt the Captain's judgment. Suddenly the worn carpet, the patriotic decor hanging on the walls, and the dank smell of 40-year-old car-siding churned her stomach.

"In case you were wondering, Cineste is doing really well," Bexley blurted as they sat. "It wouldn't hurt you to check in with your offspring every now and then. You know, to ensure they haven't been abducted, or nearly murdered."

Her father's lips tightened. "We're here on business."

"Right." All at once wishing she'd turned him away, Bexley straightened her spine and closed Temperance's file that she'd thrown together the night before. "What can I do for you, *Captain Ferguson?*"

"Hillary was assaulted."

"*What?*" Bexley's eyes shot to her step-mother. Hillary had yet to utter a syllable. Other than a deep-set scowl, which wasn't out of the ordinary, she appeared calm and unharmed. "When?"

"Last Thursday night," Hillary answered in a matter-of-fact tone. "I was at the PS Royal for our monthly Beach Ready meeting."

An assault at the city's most prestigious motel? That caught Bexley's attention. The cheapest room set guests back a cool $500 per night, keeping out the riffraff and drawing the business of some of Papaya Springs' highest society. And she hadn't been aware her stepmother was a member of the popular Beach Ready exercise cult.

Bexley's eyes volleyed between her father and Hillary. "Did you call the police?"

Her father leaned in a little closer, nostrils flaring. "No. It's a *sensitive* matter."

"Because it happened at the PS Royal?"

"Because I was *sexually* assaulted," Hillary clarified with a snarl.

While she'd never go on shopping trips or get matching tattoos with the woman who could never fill her mother's shoes, Bexley's stomach dropped. She abhorred the kind of man who thought it was acceptable to violate women. She fully met Hillary's gaze, pausing before she whispered, "I'm so sorry."

"I want you to find the man who did it," her father continued.

"And then what?" Bexley challenged. "What good will it do if you don't want the police involved?"

A grunt vibrated through her father's throat. "Let me worry about that."

Deep rage clenched Bexley's insides. He had all but abandoned Cineste. How far would her father go in the name of justice for his new wife?

Gaze softening, she addressed Hillary. "I totally understand if you're humiliated or ashamed, but you wouldn't be the first victim to feel that way.

This is a matter for the police. They're better equipped for something of this nature."

Hillary's false lashes were the only thing to move as Bexley waited for her reply. Anyone in Hillary's situation would understandably be traumatized, but this felt like something else. Bexley couldn't quite put her finger on the abnormality behind her stepmother's behavior.

"Are you saying you aren't equipped to find the criminal who violated my wife?" The Captain's venomous words sawed through Bexley's pride like a serrated knife on a raw steak. "Did I make a mistake in thinking you were competent?"

With a silent grunt, Bexley leaned back into her chair and clicked the customized pen Cineste had gifted her the first day she started working for J.J. *Be a quick-wit.* What started as an inside joke when Cineste tried to give her big sister a boost of confidence was now memorialized in an elegant gold font. It inspired Bexley to make a fast decision.

If her father was trying to goad her into the job by undermining her abilities, he was succeeding. And if he was going to treat her like a stranger, she'd simply have to do the same. Grayson would hate that she'd taken on yet another case. Finding Temperance's collar would have to take precedence, but this was something she couldn't walk away from.

With another click of the pen, she cleared her throat and met her father's imperious stare. "My rate is one hundred per hour with a non-refundable deposit of fifteen hundred, plus any expenses incurred. I expect you both to cooperate with me one hundred percent with whatever I may need. If you question my capabilities again, I will drop your case without prior notice."

With one nod, Bexley's father stood. "I'll leave a check with your secretary." His eyes lingered on her for a moment longer, lips parting as if prepared to say something more. Instead, he glanced down at Hillary while squeezing her bare shoulder. "I'm heading to the base."

Then he promptly headed out the door. *It was strictly business,* Bexley reminded herself.

The moment the door closed behind him, Hillary slid forward in her chair, mouth twisted with a grimace. "Clearly neither of us wants to be in this situation. I'm only here because your father insisted on it, and you only agreed because you're desperate for some kind of validation." Her lips spread with a sneer. "What do you say we wait a few days before we tell him that we discussed what happened in detail, and you did everything you could to find my attacker with no avail? Then we can call it good."

Bexley cocked her head. "Don't *you* want to find whoever did this to you?"

"It was traumatic enough the first time." Her eyes drifted to the corner of the room. "I have my own ways of handling what happened." Readjusting the designer handbag slung over her shoulder, Hillary slid from the chair to her feet. "Pretend you're doing your little investigation thing, and I'll make sure you're paid a fair amount."

Hillary slipped out the door. Her insistence on letting it go only fueled Bexley's curiosity.

She was hiding something. Bexley was determined to expose it.

<hr>

MID-MORNING, Temperance's driveway was a flurry of activity with service workers and vans. The madness of it all made Bexley uneasy, causing her to look over her shoulder with every noise. Security had intensified since her last visit to include a metal detector and pat-down. A beefy guard confiscated her handbag, and chided her for bringing both a stun gun and hand gun onto the property. Her heart clenched as she watched him place them inside a locker. Despite the added presence of guards, she felt naked without any way to protect herself.

After making a sweep of the seven foot wrought iron fence that surrounded the property, ensuring there weren't any spots in which the dog could've squeezed through, she headed to the backyard. There she discovered the sultry reality star directing a crew in matching white polo shirts, arranging round tables and chairs in the center of the perfectly manicured lawn.

"Planning a big shindig?" Bexley asked.

Temperance spun around with a slack expression. Though her dark hair and face appeared freshly washed, her bland gray exercise leggings and wrinkled tank top appeared unlaundered. Bexley held her breath, hoping to see Temperance's brilliant smile appear when she answered. But her expression remained stoic. "*Sí.* We will celebrate my *mamá* turning fifty."

Sadness tinged Bexley's chest. Had Dean's actions caused her to fall into a deep depression? Bexley feared she'd be crossing the line of professionalism if she asked whether or not Temperance had tried counseling. Did she have any friends or family to support her through her struggles? Aside from the caterers, the only other person Bexley spotted was a young brunette in a gauzy, pale green dress. The girl sat in the grass beside the bubbling brook with Temperance's beloved Cinderella draped across her lap. Bexley noted the dark circles under the girl's eyes and her crumpled posture as she stared blankly down at the dog, dragging a hand through its thick white fur.

Bexley motioned in their direction. "Who's that girl with Cinderella?"

"One of *Ceincienta's* handlers, Kayla," Temperance replied, turning to them with a sullen smile. "The two of them have become quite close. Poor *amor* was the most heartbroken of anyone when she disappeared."

"How long has she worked for you?"

"Since the beginning of last summer, to get her California residency. She moved to campus last week. Now she tells me she's too sad to leave my *Cenicienta* with another handler, and wants to quit her studies. But I tell her I have enough security now, she doesn't have to worry about it happening again. School is more important."

"Was she on the clock when Cinderella disappeared?"

"*Sí.* It's another reason she's so sad. She believes it was her fault."

Bexley watched as Kayla continued to methodically stroke the dog's coat. Was Temperance mistaking the girl's guilt for sadness? Could Kayla have purposely *mis*-handled the dog, hoping for a payout from her employer?

When they first discussed her case, Temperance stated that there had always been a guard stationed at the front gate, and surveillance cameras covered every square inch of the yard. Yet no one could find any suspicious activity around the time Cinderella went missing.

Bexley's eyes narrowed on Kayla. Maybe they hadn't thought to look in the most obvious place imaginable. "I'm just going to talk to her for a minute," she told Temperance as she started across the lawn.

"Kayla?"

Suspicious brown eyes met Bexley's as she neared. "Yeah. Who are you?"

"My name's Bexley. Temperance hired me to locate Cinderella's collar."

Kayla's eyes shot back down to the dog in her lap. "I already told Temperance I didn't see anything unusual that day."

Nodding, Bexley squatted down beside the girl to pet the dog's thick coat. It reminded her of an obnoxiously feminine rug her roommate had their freshman year at NYU. "How tight did you keep the collar? Was it the kind to come off easily? Is it possible it caught on something when Cinderella snuck off the property?"

"It was like pretty much any other collar—leather with a platinum buckle. Well, except for all the diamonds." The girl heaved a deep breath, eyes still fixed on the dog. "It didn't come off very easily. There's no way it would've just slipped off without getting caught on her head."

"Did you hear any loud noises that day that might've startled Cinderella? Maybe something jarring enough that she would've fit through a tight spot in the fence that normally may have been too narrow?" Remembering the sound of gunshots the night before, Bexley shuddered.

"No, there was nothing like that," Kayla mumbled. "I shouldn't have let her out of my sight." Sniffling, she buried her face in the dog's fur.

Bexley watched the girl a moment longer. From the way she clutched the dog, one would think it had almost died. "I'm going to give you my card in case you think of anything that might steer me in the right direction, okay?"

When Kayla didn't answer or remove her face from the dog's coat, Bexley tucked the card inside the messenger bag in the grass at Kayla's side before leaving the compound.

She was certain there was more to Kayla's story.

CHAPTER FOUR

Kayla Dahl was a squeaky clean 19-year-old from the lakeside city of Albert Lea, Minnesota. She'd earned an academic scholarship to Papaya Springs College. Bexley was unable to find any sort of criminal record from Kayla's past, neither as a juvenile nor an adult—not even a simple traffic violation or an underage consumption. The youngest of two girls to Jana and Terry Dahl, an elementary teacher and a crop farmer, spent her formative years working for a maternal aunt who trained championship dogs. Every summer since the age of ten, Kayla had shown her own canines at the local county fair. Throughout her senior high, she had received numerous rewards for charity work with various foundations. She was one of the leaders of her church's youth group, co-captain of the cheerleading squad, and her school's Homecoming queen. She'd lived in Temperance's servant quarters since June 2nd of the prior year, and had just moved into Newman Hall in the center of campus. Her pre-veterinary classes were scheduled to start the following week.

Bexley clicked to exit the class schedule and shut down her laptop. From where she sat—not in her office, but *figuratively*—Kayla didn't seem like the type to kidnap her employer's dog for money. But experience had taught Bexley to never assume anything about anyone. *Ever.*

Later that evening, she tailed the college freshman from Temperance's estate to PSC. Kayla parked her mother's old mid-sized sedan still bearing Minnesota license plates in the lot outside her dorm, and spent the better part of an hour inside as the sun sunk into the horizon. She re-emerged in a short floral dress, shoulder-length hair in loose spirals, makeup applied to perfection. Arm-in-arm with a platinum blonde in nearly identical attire, they walked two well-illuminated campus blocks to a colossal two-story Tudor house that proudly displayed the Greek letters KKΔ above the double front doors. Smack-dab in the center of Sorority Row.

"Yay, Kappa Kappa Delta," Bexley cheered, watching from behind her camera's zoom lens inside the loaner SUV as the girls approached the arched entrance along with a small hoard of more girls. "Welcome to Rush Week, ladies. Be sure to check your self-respect at the door."

Greek life was as foreign to Bexley as kumquats —she was aware they both existed, but the details were sketchy. What little she knew of sorority practices, she'd gleaned from classmates at NYU, and animated retellings of first-hand experiences from Kiersten, her high school bestie. It was behind those very same doors of Kappa Kappa Delta that Kiersten had learned to transform literally anything into a costume for outlandishly themed parties, and mastered the Sorority Squat.

Once Kayla and her friend were ushered in through red and silver streamers hanging over the threshold, Bexley slipped out from the loaner SUV and crossed the street to the property, using a wall of fragrant gardenia bushes as cover. She crept along the side of the house, emerging in a vast backyard of perfectly manicured Kentucky grass and upscale lawn furniture among an outdoor kitchen. Peals of laughter rumbled from inside the brightly lit mansion, and red and silver balloons littered the abandoned yard.

Bexley moved in closer, peering into the basement windows. Like something out of a horror movie, dozens of girls gathered in a room dressed up as some kind of Satanic temple done in shades of red and silver, forming a circle around a cluster of candles. Kayla was wedged in near the door, squeezed between a fold of fake satin drapery and a very solid-looking security door.

Unlike the joyous sounds of a party taking shape on the main floor, these girls were painfully somber and remained dead silent. It would appear that the girls were taking part in some kind of strange ritual.

Just how involved were the Kappa Kappa Deltas in hazing? Enough that they'd expect a recruit to steal something extremely valuable to prove her loyalty?

Red and silver glitter. Kappa Kappa Deltas' house colors.

Cinderella had been covered in red and silver glitter.

INVITING Kiersten to join them for dinner last minute didn't phase Grayson in the slightest. It was common practice since Bexley's return to the area, and Kiersten's self-proclaimed status as a spinster. The three friends had effortlessly slipped back into a routine that strengthened their bond even more than before. Per usual, their stunning fashion designer friend breezed into Grayson's kitchen without knocking. She was smartly dressed in one of her own designs with a bottle of wine in hand and a mouthful of rumors. As soon as she squeezed her thin arms around Bexley, she blurted, "Did you hear they aren't renewing Temperance Rose's show for another season?"

"Can you blame her? I wouldn't want a camera in my face after all she's been through. She's having a hard time processing the fact that she was in love with a murderer."

Kiersten's eyebrows shot upward. "You say that like the two of you are still in touch."

Bexley turned to watch her dark-haired hunk of a boyfriend expertly trim a Brussel sprout behind the island, thick arms flexing as they twisted and turned. "We are…on occasion."

Grayson's job required him to stay in shape, warranting his strict dedication to the gym, but he had started watching what he ate, and had bulked up considerably. The fibers of his old Nirvana T-shirt stretched to their limit over his impressive pectoral muscles.

"I'd give anything to have a little eye candy cooking for me at the end of a long day." Kiersten whispered with a breathy sigh. "You're lucky I consider him to be a brother."

Grayson glanced up, catching them in the act of ogling, and shared a lighthearted grin with Bexley. All too often, she forgot to stop and smell the sandalwood. They had a good thing going. Maybe it was time to give in.

He arched a thick eyebrow in Kiersten's direction. "Did you find the Pinot Noir I told you about? You'll never wanna eat salmon again without it."

Kiersten crossed the kitchen, setting the bottle on the counter beside him. "Snagged the last one on the shelf." She regarded him with a teasing grin. "And something tells me I'm not going to want to eat anyone else's salmon again after sampling yours."

The two women assisted in preparing the meal by setting the table, and throwing together a Cesar salad. While feasting on Grayson's scrumptious salmon and roasted vegetables, they sipped the

Pinot and caught each other up on their day as Eddie Veddar's deep voice rocked from the speakers. After the plates had been cleared and they gathered in the backyard around the fire pit, Bexley finally found an opening to casually address the reason she'd invited Kiersten.

"This morning they brought a girl in on prostitution charges that I would've sworn was only sixteen," Grayson told them as Bexley settled back against his chest. "Turns out she was twenty-one. Made me feel ancient."

"I know what you mean," Kiersten said. "Our PR department brought in someone with a four year degree to manage the social media accounts for a new clothing line, but I swear she doesn't look old enough to have graduated college. Kids in their early twenties are starting to appear disgustingly youthful. I refuse to believe it's because we're getting older."

Bexley cleared her throat. "Speaking of college students…I drove by PSC campus on my way home and noticed a higher than usual infestation of girls walking around in tiny sundresses. Either the sororities are starting to rush, or there's a disconcerting invasion of Stepford wives in Papaya Springs."

"It's rush week." Kiersten set her chin on the

palm of her upturned hand. "Ah, memories. I can practically taste the naivety of new blood walking through those doors."

"Is rushing really as bad as the rumors?" Bexley prodded. "I know hazing is illegal, but they must still do *some* questionable things to new recruits behind closed doors, right?"

"I can't speak for all sororities, but rushing with Kappa Kappa Delta is nothing like Hollywood portrays. It mostly involves a lot of intimidation and mind games." Her expression became animated. "Then there's a candle-lit initiation ceremony where everyone wears black robes and drinks red wine from a goblet with drops of everyone's blood. It's pretty tame. They don't force you to drink alcohol against your will, slap you with a paddle, or anything remotely barbaric. *That's* the kind of hazing that's illegal."

Bexley narrowed her eyes. "Is that all? I swear I remember you once saying something about having to perform a scavenger hunt. Would it be unheard of to make potential pledges steal something expensive?"

Kiersten twisted in her lawn chair to face Bexley head-on. "Wow. That question felt incredibly specific. This wouldn't have something to do with an active case you're working on, would it?"

"Would you believe me if I told you it didn't?" Bexley asked, flashing an innocent smile.

Kiersten rolled her eyes. "Bex, I wouldn't believe you if you told me the ocean was blue."

Grayson shifted in his seat. "Well, technically…"

Bending in closer, Kiersten dismissed him with a wave of her hand, her lips quirked with amusement. "Just between the three of us, I may have known a legendary recruit who once commandeered the dean's car long enough to tick an item off a scavenger hunt. For the record, the car was eventually returned without a scratch, so you could technically say it was *borrowed*."

Exchanging a look with Grayson over her shoulder, Bexley's pulse quickened. "So what else goes on during sorority week? Don't they have a bunch of parties? Would there be one…say…tomorrow night?"

"Wait a minute." Kiersten tilted her head, eyes narrowed. "You're not planning to bring the Deltas down for something serious or anything, are you? I can't in good conscience offer my sisters up for slaughter."

Bexley glanced back at Kiersten. "I'm not looking for trouble...I swear. I simply want to recover something misplaced by a client."

With a little sigh, Kiersten's shoulders rolled forward. "Thursday's their designated nacho night. It's really just another excuse for the sorority to entertain all students at PSC. They love to throw a good party, even though it's against official house rules to drink. The *real* parties don't get going until later at night."

THE SMELL of bacon roused Bexley from a light sleep. She stumbled blurry-eyed into Grayson's kitchen, finding the hunky detective humming while scrambling eggs on the stovetop. Best of all, he was wearing nothing more than a pair of striped boxer briefs.

"Not that I'm complaining, because this beats the hell out of waking to find presents under the tree when I was a pig-tailed rug-rat, but shouldn't you be at work, busting skulls and taking names?"

Grayson grinned back at her over one broad shoulder. "My lieutenant ordered me to take a few days off. HR said I've been putting in too much overtime working with the FBI on Halliwell's case. I was thinking we could head up to Napa tomorrow—spend a few days with my parents."

"You know I'm right in the middle of a case."

"It's a *dog collar*, Bex, and you're probably right about the sorority having stolen it as a prank. That girl likely had no idea of its true value. I bet they'll return it over the weekend."

Irritation ticked up her spine. "Since it's an inanimate object, you're suggesting I simply neglect my job and step away to let the issue resolve itself?"

He spun to face her, spatula in hand. "I'm saying you should spend the weekend reconnecting with your man while getting to know the people who raised him over bottles of your favorite wines." His full lips tilted with an adorable grin. "When's the last time we spent more than a handful of hours together?"

She pulled the stool out and slipped into the seat, heaving with frustration. "It does sound amazing, but I really can't this weekend. My father and step-monster stopped by to see me yesterday. They said Hillary was assaulted."

Grayson's mouth sagged open, then snapped shut. "What? When did it happen? Did they call it in?"

"You know The Captain. He wouldn't want his dirty laundry aired. She was staying at the Royal for one of those crazy, body-conscience housewives' meetings when it happened. They asked me to look into it. Well my father did, anyway. Hillary wants me to pretend for my father's sake, and let it go."

"She's probably scared of the repercussions that could come with her accusations. It's a common reaction with victims." He turned to the stove to remove the pan of eggs, and turn off the gas burner. "You should encourage her to see a counselor."

"Maybe, but in the meantime I'm going to try to see if I can find this guy. If I don't, it'll only confirm to my father that I'm a big fat failure."

Grayson solemnly shook his head as he rounded the island to slip a warm hand inside her hair. "Your father's opinion of you doesn't count. Anyone else who knows you believes in your abilities."

"Sure about that? You might want to consult with Dean Halliwell and Richard Warren."

"They haven't found anything to indicate you were wrong about Warren, and you caught Halliwell with a shrine of victims' shoes. Nothing about that constitutes a failure, Bex. You don't have anything to prove to anyone—*especially* not your old man. You've said it yourself…the only way he'd be proud was if you had joined the Navy, or had been born a boy."

Moisture burned behind Bexley's eyes. With a lick of irritation, she blinked the tears away. "I just want him to be proud for a change."

"Forget him," Grayson said, massaging his fingers against her scalp. "Forget *your job*. Just for a few days. No one deserves time off more than you—you've been running yourself ragged. I could probably get a couple extra days so we could fly to Maui. My mom has been begging us to come visit their new timeshare. Besides, summer is practically over, and we haven't spent a single day together at the beach."

Leaning into his touch, she sighed dreamily. She hadn't been to Hawaii since preschool when her father was temporarily stationed at Pearl Harbor. They lived in a cramped little apartment over-looking a golf course. It was the happiest she remembered her mom being at any point in her childhood. She constantly told Bexley not many people could say they once lived in paradise. "You had me at Aloha."

Grayson's fingers stilled. "Does that mean you'll go?"

She wanted to, more than anything. "Can I get back to you with an answer later tonight? I want to run by the Royal to see what they know about Hillary's stay, and later swing by the sorority house one last time to see if I can find anything more on the collar." Looking into his russet colored eyes, she hooked her fingers around Grayson's bicep. "J.J. knows a trick to get great deals on last minute flights. I can ask him to hook us up."

"Do whatever it takes." Grayson bent to brush his soft lips over hers, and backed away with a grin. "Even if we don't go anywhere, one way or another I'm going to find a way to get you in a bikini this weekend."

"That could be a little awkward if we end up touring wineries with your parents."

With a husky laugh, he dropped a kiss in her hair. "At this point, I don't care where we are when it happens. I'll take whatever I can get."

CHAPTER FIVE

According to the social calendar listed on Kappa Kappa Delta's website, Nacho Night wasn't set to begin until mid-evening. As Kayla was scheduled to spend the day at Temperance's, working with Cinderella, Bexley had time to both rummage through her closet at the condo for the outfit from her last case, and look into her step-mother's case before the Greek festivities resumed.

The twin towers of the Papaya Springs Royal twinkled over the city in the cresting sunlight like a fortress. Bexley rolled her eyes when snubbed by the doorman. She didn't need some overpaid door jam looking right through her like she wasn't worthy of stepping foot in what was essentially a grossly over-priced brothel. Successful businessmen in Papaya

Springs used the motel as a place to meet prostitutes, and the PS Royal staff protected the reputation of their guests at all costs. If they knew of Hillary's allegations, all hell would break loose.

She made her way toward the reception desk, and was given a firm nod by a glossy-haired woman with a face so plastic that Bexley was convinced if she took the woman outside, she would melt. "How may I help you?"

"Hi!" Bexley sang, placing the palms of her hands on the marble desk and flashing a plastic smile of her own. "You're not going to believe this, but my mom stayed here last week, and she just now remembered this was the last place she saw her diamond earrings given to her by my father. She's *such* a ditz! Any chance I could search the room?"

"If they were truly left behind, one of our maids would've turned them in by now."

Work with me here, lady, Bexley thought. She lifted one shoulder. "Maybe they fell into a hard-to-reach crevice."

The woman's cutting cornflower blue eyes slitted, and her thin lips quirked with a scowl. It was surprising to see her surgically altered features allowed her more flexibility than Bexley would've guessed. "May I see some identification?"

"Of course!" Bexley rifled through her bag, silently chiding herself for not holding onto her expired driver's license bearing her maiden name. She froze, gritting her teeth and throwing the women a pleading look. "I forgot my wallet at home."

"I'm sorry, but Papaya Springs Royal is a five-star establishment. We didn't earn our reputation by giving just *anyone* off the streets access to one of our rooms."

It didn't seem Bexley would get anywhere with the woman, so she gave up the fight. "Maybe I'll give my mom a call—see if she can come meet me."

"That would be preferable," the woman replied with a smug smile.

Bexley patted the desk between them, knowing it would irk the woman to have her hand prints smudged all over the tempered glass. "You have a *lovely* day."

She'd find another way to access Hillary's room, and search for any clues as to what had gone down that night. But first, she figured she'd ask around to see what information she could dig up about Hillary and her monthly meetings.

As she passed through the bowels of the motel

toward the Royal's 5-star restaurant renowned for lobster and ribeye, her phone rang from her handbag. It pained her to answer an unknown number, but it had become a necessity with her job.

"Hey, Bexley, it's Alex," his deep voice rumbled. "Hope you don't mind that I swiped your number off your sister's phone."

Her stomach dropped. "Is Cineste okay?"

"Yeah, she's fine. I knew she'd have questions if I straight up asked her for your number. I just wanted to check in…you know, after what happened the other night. Knowing someone wants you six feet under can really mess with a person's head."

Bexley ground her teeth together, and ducked into a nearby restroom. "I appreciate your discretion," she whispered while checking the stalls to make sure she was alone. "But I'm fine, I swear. It's not like someone hasn't wished me dead before."

"So you *haven't* purposely avoided coming back home the past two nights because of what happened?"

"You mean other than the fact that a murderous asshole clearly knows where I live?"

She studied her reflection in the mirror, suddenly made aware that lack of sleep and appetite had caught up to her. There was a light dusting of dark patches beneath her green eyes, and the bones in her shoulders appeared sharp beneath her skin. Not only that, but her olive complexion was noticeably paled, and her mahogany hair didn't have as much luster as usual. Is that the reason Grayson was pushing so hard for time away?

Her tongue clicked against her teeth. "Sorry, Alex, but I don't see how this is any of your business."

"You're the most important person in Cineste's life right now, and she's becoming the most important person in mine. Neither of us has much for family, so I figure we have to look out for each other."

A laugh stuck in her throat. How had Bexley and her sister both managed to get involved with sensitive men? And why was he making his short-lived relationship with Cineste sound so serious?

"That's…ah…sweet of you, but it takes more than a few stray bullets to get my hackles up." *You know, like that time when a sociopath with a hobby of killing brunettes tried to choke the life from me with his bare hands.* "I'm right in the middle of a job, so I really need to get going."

"I just wanted to remind you that I've been

through a lot myself between my family and training with the Navy, so if you ever wanna talk, I'd probably be able to at least empathize with what you're going through."

She gritted her teeth and said, "Thanks," then ended the call.

After consulting her wretched reflection one last time, she returned to the hall. It was easy to locate the restaurant once she followed the rich aroma of roast beef. Spotless windows stretched from the blood-red carpet to a ceiling several stories high, providing a spectacular view of the city that would surely improve drastically once darkness fell. Modern stools of ivory leather and polished steel lined the bar beneath a mammoth chandelier adorned in crystals.

Bexley sidled up at the center of the generous stone-topped bar. The towering, fit man approached her with a wide, flirtatious smile. He was boyishly handsome, somewhere in his mid 20s, and exuded charm. He made the slim-fitting button down and narrow tie more appealing than a tuxedo.

"I'm Gage," his deep voice rumbled. "What can I get you, sweetheart?"

It was a completely different reception from

those she'd received from his colleagues, but she supposed his job required him to butter up for tips. Either that or he was a serious player. "Will you judge me if I order alcohol at this early hour, Gage?"

Deep dimples pressed his cheeks. "Haven't you heard that saying, the customer's always right?"

"In that case, hit me up with a diet soda."

"Wow. You're a breath of fresh air. Keep that up and I'll have to insist you have my children." Gage wiggled his eyebrows as he headed for the soda machine. "What brings a fine woman like yourself into our fine establishment today?"

Haven't you heard that flattery won't get you anywhere, Mr. Tall, Dark, and Sleazy? Bexley thought. "I'm supposed to meet my sister, but she must be running late." It was far easier to claim Hillary as a sibling rather than trying to explain why someone nearly her own age was technically a parental figure. "Maybe you know her—this is her usual hangout. Well, at least once every month for the Beach Ready meetings."

"Yeah? BR's an excellent program. It helped me drop a quick ten pounds for a walk-on role last winter. I didn't know they had monthly meetings here."

"Really?" Bexley sat a little taller. Over the past year, she'd had her suspicions that Hillary kept a lot of things from her father, so it wasn't exactly a revelation. But faking monthly meetings would be a significant factor in finding her attacker. What else was Hillary lying about? Had she even been at the Royal when the alleged assault happened? "How long have you worked here?"

"I guess it's been a little over five years by now, but I usually work the day shift, so I don't always know what's going on in the conference halls." His dimpled smile returned as he looked up from the soda machine. "What's your sister's name?"

"Hillary Ferguson."

He made his way back over to Bexley, setting her soda on the bar. "Doesn't ring a bell."

"She's around six feet tall, ash-blond hair down to her elbows, chest out to here…" Bexley cupped her hands out in front of her, grossly exaggerating her step-mother's augmented chest.

"Don't stop now." He grinned and leaned in, setting an elbow on the bar between them. "You're describing my dream girl."

Bexley hoped he didn't detect her slight gag. "Hold on, I have a picture." She dug for her smart phone, and quickly pulled up her step-mother's most recent profile picture on social media. The seductive selfie was more appropriate for a dating site with the caption *"nowhere near single but still willing to mingle."*

"Her hair's a little longer now," Bexley explained, handing her phone to Gage. "Otherwise she hasn't changed."

Upon first seeing the picture, his eyes slightly bulged from his head. *"She's* your sister?"

"Yeah. You know her?"

"Nah." He handed the phone back to Bexley, awkwardly shifting his stance and looking away. "It just…you two look nothing alike."

"That's because we're *step*-sisters." She waited for him to look back her way, but he began polishing another glass. "Are you *sure* you haven't seen her around? Maybe if you'd take another look—"

"Haven't seen her. I'd definitely remember a knockout like that." He cleared his throat before meeting Bexley's stare. "Unless you need anything else, I have other patrons who need my attention." His smile was weak and insincere as he dried his hands and sauntered away.

Suspicion stewed in Bexley's gut. In her somewhat limited experience of performing investigative duties, there was only one good reason why a person would lie about knowing someone.

* * *

THE BARTENDER'S shift ended at six. He exited through the employee door in the alley behind the motel precisely ten minutes after six, and slid behind the wheel of a midnight black Camaro. Bexley kept several cars' distance between them as he headed out of Papaya Springs, and took the 405 toward L.A.

While the flirtatious bartender served closeted alcoholics and adulterers at the famed motel, Bexley spent her day digging into his background. The never-married 23-year-old from Colorado had relocated from Denver to Papaya Springs after losing his job, apartment, and girlfriend all within a matter of days. A criminal history check showed possession of drug paraphernalia as a minor, and an indecent exposure the same night. After high school, he attended college in Denver for a semester before dropping out to bartend at a swanky nightclub downtown. Bexley called his former employer, pretending to be a potential new employer to Gage, and was given more information than she'd ever want. Turns out the manager was an ex-girlfriend of Gage's. She'd been cheated on so many times that she wasn't afraid to dish the dirt.

"If you ask me, he's too stupid to understand 'table service' is merely a term used in the service industry," the woman had said in a notably cold, bitter voice. "Apparently he believed it had something to do with sexual favors performed on the tables in the VIP lounge." Bexley could picture the woman's fingers turning white as she gripped the phone, teeth clenched. "If you're foolish enough to hire him, you'll wanna have the place bleached every night so his STDs don't spread."

Bexley couldn't imagine the woman had relayed the same message when he submitted his application to the Royal. Part of Bexley enjoyed the fact that he had pulled a fast one on the city's finest, while another part wondered what his unsavory reputation meant for Hillary. Was Gage the type who was so used to getting what he wanted from women that he would force himself on someone who refused? Either way, would Bexley feel sorry for her?

The Camaro veered off onto an exit on the south side of Los Angeles. Bexley followed him a dozen blocks or so to a seedy motel with peeling paint, broken windows, and a long-since abandoned pool. The sports car parked beneath a sign in which burned out neon spelled "Big Dick's Inn."

"*Someone's* compensating for something," Bexley muttered to herself.

Gage climbed out in aviator sunglasses, taking a slow visual sweep of his surroundings before heading toward a room on the first floor. He merely knocked once before the door swung open. A woman's arm wearing only a sparkling cuff bracelet grabbed his tie and yanked him inside. The door slammed shut behind them.

"Now we're talkin'," Bexley muttered, sitting taller in her seat.

Though she was unable to see anything beyond the jewelry and eager arm, she had a theory behind the woman's identity. Retrieving her phone from her SUV's center console, Bexley queued a song on her streaming service, then dialed Big Dick's Inn on her burner phone.

"Big Dick's Inn," a voice drawled in a southern accent. "What can I do you for?"

"Hi, can you patch me into my mom's room?" Bexley squinted, reading the number of the room Gage had slipped into. "She said she's in number fourteen."

"Sure thing, sugar."

The phone rang several times. Then: "Hello?" Her step-mom's voice brimmed with impatience. "Who's this?"

"Good afternoon," Bexley greeted in a grossly overdone southern accent. "This is the front desk of Big Dick's callin'. Would you please move your black sports car to another parking spot? We hired an electrician to replace the bulbs on our sign, and that car is *right* where his boom truck needs to go."

"Sure, whatever."

"Oh, and ma'am? One more thing." Bexley played the queued song from her personal phone, letting Sting deliver her final message.

"*...Every step you take, I'll be watching you.*"

Before the count of five, the motel room's ratty curtain was pushed aside. Wearing a black negligee, Bexley's step-mom peered out the window, corded phone pressed to her ear. "Is this Bexley, you nosy little bitch? What I do with my life is none of your goddamn—"

Bexley ended the call, and promptly dialed her father. For the first time in ages, he answered instead of letting it go to voicemail. "Did you find something?" he barked.

Good day to you, too, Dad. Bexley swallowed hard

as she quickly planned how she'd break the news. Was her father capable of shedding a tear, or would his wife's indiscretion merely fuel him with rage? A jaded side of her wanted to drag the conversation out to make him suffer, maybe even sweat a little inside his meticulously-ironed uniform.

"Did Hillary tell you she was assaulted because she contracted an STD?" she asked.

A long length of silence followed her question.

"Did she tell you that?"

"No, it's just a hunch. After you left my office, she told me not to look into her alleged assault. I believe it's because she's having an affair with a young bartender from the Royal by the name of Gage Colton. Those 'meetings' she claimed she was attending don't exist. They were merely an alibi. She's with him now at a motel in South L.A., although I don't believe they'll be here much longer. Do you want me to get pictures, or—"

"Your word will suffice," he replied, his voice suddenly soft. "It seems your instincts about Hillary were right all along. Your mother never would've done this to me."

Two muted beeps sounded in Bexley's ear. He'd ended the call.

CHAPTER SIX

Moments after Bexley pulled into Grayson's driveway, the door on her loaner flew open before she had a chance to reach for the handle. Heart leaping into her throat, she squeezed her eyes shut, expecting another attack. Visions of Dean Halliwell's twisted grin, and bullets whizzing over her head came to her in the darkness. All at once, she couldn't breathe.

"Aloha, beautiful."

With the sound of Grayson's deep voice, she released her breath and opened her eyes, hand spread over her chest. If she didn't learn to relax, she'd die of a heart attack before the ripe old age of thirty. She at least needed to reach for her gun.

Grayson wrapped gentle fingers around her

wrist. "Whoa, you alright? I didn't mean to scare you."

"You didn't." She recovered quickly with a smile before sliding out from the driver's seat to kiss him softly. "Don't tell me you waited all day on the front step for me to return."

He flashed a charming smile that she could feel in the pit of her stomach. "Too romantic?"

"Sad, like a puppy waiting for its owner to come home." She poked a finger into his rib cage. "Definitely not the actions of the valiant detective who swept me off my feet."

He locked his arms around her, one eyebrow raised. "I swept you off your feet, eh?"

"Cockiness isn't flattering either."

"What if I told you that we're hopping on a plane for Maui first thing tomorrow morning?" he whispered with a seductive rumble, the words tickling her ear. "Is that gallant enough for you?"

Her heart thumped with a deep rush of disappointment. "I told you I'd give you a final answer some time tonight." She broke free from him, scowling. "You didn't make arrangements already, did you?"

Wiping at his day-old stubble, he looked away. "You were right. J.J. was able to get us a heck of a deal, and my parents were more than happy to meet us at their timeshare."

"Grayson…*seriously*." She leaned up against the hood of the loaner and sighed. "I'm too tired to fight with you, and I still have to run by the sorority later. This day has taken a lot out of me already."

His eyes met hers. "Did you have any luck at the Royal?"

"You could say that. Turns out step-mother dearest is having an affair. I caught her with a young lover at a motel near L.A."

"Have you told your father?"

"Yeah, and he didn't exactly seem shocked. At least he didn't demand physical proof. Believe it or not, he said he'd take me for my word."

"Coming from him, that's one better than an 'atta girl'." Grayson kissed her forehead, letting his lips linger. "How about you take a bath while I finish making dinner? Then we'll discuss our plans for the weekend like civilized adults over a glass of wine before you head out."

She was sold on the idea of soaking in warm suds. Although after witnessing her stepmother's repugnant behavior, she would've preferred a bath in bleach.

THE SORORITY HOUSE was bustling with drunk students by the time Bexley waltzed in through the open front doors just before midnight. Not only had she needed the time to swing by her condo and pack a bag for their weekend away, she'd decided it would be best to show up fashionably late, especially since she was flying solo. She nearly jumped out of her skin when greeted by two girls with identically over-the-top smiles and *"we're going to eat you alive"* eyes. Not to mention they both stunk of booze and wavered on their feet.

"Welcome to Kappa Kappa Delta!"

At a loss for words, Bexley simply pointed at them with a cheesy grin before she continued further inside the well-furnished house. She had assumed "nacho night" was merely an excuse for a gathering, and was surprised to see there was actually a depleted nacho bar set up in a long dining room. She *wasn't* surprised when she noticed a bunch of scantily clad girls, including several in grass skirts with bikinis and artificial leis strung around their necks. She couldn't even guess how they had decided on a tropical theme for nacho night, but at least it made the Kappa Kappa Deltas easy to spot.

Though Bexley had swung by Kiersten's house for a sorority-worthy makeover that included a pound of makeup products and a honey-blond wig, she felt sorely out of place. She couldn't imagine a single scenario that would involve her willingly subjecting herself to this way of life.

She waited in the line leading up to a tiki bar, plastic blue cup they had given her at the door in hand. A couple of drunk guys horsing around behind her knocked Bexley off her feet. She went flying toward a raven-haired beauty with darkly tanned skin who smelled like fruit. The two women braced arms to prevent a collision. The girl started to giggle.

"Oh my god, I'm so sorry!" Bexley said, bending to retrieve her cup.

The girl continued to giggle, palm of one hand held up. "Clearly it wasn't your fault. It's just a good thing I didn't have my drink yet, or you'd be painted in coconut rum." She then offered her hand, slender with long, perfectly-manicured fingers. "Hi, I'm Maci."

"Celeste," Bexley improvised, shaking her hand. She motioned to the girl's hot-pink, triangle-style bikini top, and green grass skirt adorned with silk flowers. "Are you a Delta?"

Maci bobbed her head. "Sure am…I'm the VP. Have you considered pledging with the Deltas before?"

"I don't know…I'm a fifth-year senior, so it's probably a little late for that," Bexley replied with a nervous laugh. "What's it like?"

"OMG, it's so friggen' awesome!" Maci grabbed Bexley's arm as her dark eyes lit excitedly. "You get to wear matching outfits for special occasions like tonight, and learn secret handshakes. We even have our own lingo! You make friends for life—everyone puts sisterhood first! Seriously, you're totally missing out!"

"But don't sororities like this make you do weird stuff to get in?"

Maci's smile faltered. "Weird stuff? Like what?"

"You know." Bexley twisted the ends of the wig between her fingers. "I've heard you have to do these tasks, like…pranks."

"I don't know who you've been talking to, but it's nothing too serious." Maci shrugged as they stepped closer to the bar. "If you mean hazing, they stopped doing that kind of thing ages ago…like when *my mom* went here."

A tall, fairly muscular guy with great wavy brown hair clasped his thick arms around Maci from behind. "Guess who?"

With a squeak, Maci spun around and the couple kissed passionately with tongues and groping hands. Deciding she wasn't getting anywhere with Maci anyway, Bexley maneuvered around them to have her drink filled.

Rap music blasted non-stop as Bexley wandered around the party for the better part of an hour, pretending to sip from the cup of booze that smelled akin to gasoline. She thoroughly studied the overall mood of every last guest in attendance. Nothing felt amiss, and everyone seemed to be enjoying themselves. She decided it was as good a time as any to give herself a tour of the house.

In a short hallway that connected the kitchen and party room, a platinum blonde curled up on a velvet settee with her knees tucked against her chest, full drink on a nearby ledge. She wore the same grass skirt as Maci with a modest royal blue bikini top. Her expression was considerably sullen compared to the partygoers in the next room, and a large scrape scabbed over the tip of her nose and the apples of her cheeks.

"Everything okay?" Bexley asked, stopping beside the girl.

Beautiful blue eyes peered up at her, glossy and unfocused. "Yeah, I'm fine." She sniffled before setting her chin on her knees.

Sensing something was seriously off with the girl, Bexley remained in place. She easily could've been drugged, and Bexley wasn't about to leave her alone when she was clearly vulnerable. "You must be a Delta too. I'm Celeste, by the way."

The girl hesitated before flashing a timid smile. "Violet."

"This place seems a little…intense."

Violet snorted. "You should try pledging with them."

"I thought about it once…for a millisecond." Bexley sat at the end of the settee. "Is it that bad?"

Eyes darting toward the party room, Violet whispered, "Can you keep a secret?"

"Yeah, of course," Bexley said, nodding.

"This place is bad news." Her tense gaze returned to Bexley. "They don't go by the rules. It's like they think they're above them or something."

A warm tingle ran down Bexley's spine. She was actually getting somewhere for a change. "What do you mean?"

"The way they make you pledge…it's demeaning and…*wrong*."

Hand on the girl's bicep, Bexley whispered, "What did they make you do, Violet? What happened to your face?"

Wiping at a tear on her cheek, Violet shook her head several times. "If they found out I told someone…"

"I won't tell anyone, I swear."

"I don't even know you!" Violet snapped, scooting away from her.

"You're right, but I'm someone who could help."

Violet remained rigid, lips pinched together. Whatever was going on with the sorority had to be colossal if the girl was too afraid of the consequences to speak up.

"No offense," Bexley said, "but if it's so bad, why are you still here? Why don't you leave?"

"One of my best friends…she got herself into… *something* because of them. I'm trying to help her… help her find a way out. She…*borrowed* something from someone important…she thought she was only proving to the Deltas how badly she wanted it…she totally planned to take it back. They had other ideas." Tears splashed onto Violet's knees as she spoke. "Kayla had no idea they were going to keep it! It's not fair if she gets into trouble!"

Bingo. "Violet, this is important. Look at me." Once she had the girl's full attention, she asked, "Are you talking about Temperance Rose's dog and its collar?"

The girl's mouth fell open and back shut as she scrambled to her feet. "Who are you?"

"Violet?" a sharp voice interrupted. "What's going on?"

Bexley's heart hammered when she discovered they had company. Maci and Kayla made up two-thirds of the mob standing over them.

"Who are you?" the third girl, a redhead, demanded.

"Her name is *Celeste*," said Maci. "She almost knocked me on my ass while I was waiting for a drink."

"Her name isn't Celeste, it's *Bexley Squires,*" Kayla intervened. Her eyes blazed on Bexley. "Nice disguise. What're you doing here? Did you follow me?"

The redhead gasped. "Wait. You're that nosy bitch who landed my daddy in jail for sleeping with a couple of hookers!" she seethed through gritted teeth. "What the hell are you doing in *my* house?"

Bexley met Kayla's stare. "I know about Cinderella's collar."

Kayla's complexion drained to a sickly white, and her eyes fell downward.

"I'm not here to lay blame on anyone," Bexley continued. "I just want to help Temperance, and finish the job she hired me to do. You and I both know she's been through a lot. Don't you want to see her happy?"

With parted lips, Kayla's gaze swung back to Bexley. "I—"

The redhead wedged herself between Bexley and Kayla. "We don't know anything about a collar!"

"Alicia—" Kayla interjected.

"She's trespassing on private property!" Alicia snapped back. "I don't know who you think you are, but I'm not going to let you pin bogus charges on us the way you did with my father and all his friends. If you don't remove yourself from the premises immediately, I'm calling campus security. We'll see how *you* like spending a little quality time behind bars."

Bexley took a step closer toward the girl. "You can threaten me all you want, but I'm not giving up until that collar is returned to Temperance."

The girl's blood-red lips parted with a menacing smile. "We'll see about that. Maci, call security. *Now.*"

As Maci obediently pulled her phone from the depths of her tiny bikini top, Bexley started walking backwards in the direction of the front door. "Don't bother. I've seen enough." Then she held Kayla's dumfounded expression. "Think about how you want this to end…for you *and Temperance.*"

THE GENTLE RING of Bexley's phone alarm ripped her from a deep sleep. She'd returned to Grayson's sometime around 2 a.m., and slipped into bed without disrupting him, but the events of the night prevented her from sleeping for hours. She'd told Grayson she'd spend the weekend in Maui if she didn't come across anything dire at the party. But Violet seemed terrified of what would happen to her if she spilled the sorority's secrets. What kind of dangerous games were they playing? Was it serious enough that it needed Bexley's immediate attention?

Stretching her limbs around her, she found the

other side of the bed cold and empty. It wasn't unusual for Grayson to get up before her, but the house was quiet. She figured he'd be cranking his favorite Beach Boys tunes while packing for their trip.

"Grayson?"

She snagged his faded Pearl Jam t-shirt from the bench at the end of their bed and slipped it over her head before tiptoeing into the kitchen. The coffee maker light was on and the small pot was half empty. Grayson's favorite mug sat beside the sink, still steaming and filled to the brim. Unease slithered through her mind. *Since when would Grayson leave behind a good cup of coffee?*

Retrieving her gun from her handbag by the front door, she headed toward the garage, and cracked the fire-retardant door open. There was an odd stillness among the shadows.

Then the silence was breached by a soft rustling. *Someone was in the garage.*

"Come out with your hands up where I can see them!" she called out.

A loud mechanical noise stirred in the dark. She took aim at the source and pulled the trigger. The din of the shot in the confined space was deafening.

Bexley realized her mistake as the garage door lifted just enough to light her surroundings. She had shot Grayson's garage door motor.

"Holy shit, Bex!" Grayson hollered, emerging from his black work sedan. "What in the hell are you doing?"

"I saw your untouched coffee…then…I heard something and thought…it's time you replace that motor." Embarrassment warmed her cheeks as she lowered the weapon to her side, eyeing Grayson's suit and tie. "I know it's been awhile since you've been on vacation, but I'm pretty sure that's the wrong kind of suit."

"I was hoping I wouldn't wake you." Rubbing at the back of his neck, he glanced up at the broken garage door motor. "I'm sorry, but we might have to reschedule the trip. I have to head into the station."

Bexley clenched her jaw rather than pointing out the fact that he had berated *her* for choosing her job over spending quality time together. "For what reason?"

"Lieutenant Baker's daughter was brought into the ER for alcohol poisoning about an hour ago. It doesn't look good…she's in a coma. He asked me to help him piece together what happened, and find out who gave her the booze."

At least he has a valid excuse, she thought. "I wasn't aware the Lieutenant had a family."

"He purposely keeps her identity a secret so she's not a target to his enemies. I don't know a whole lot about Violet myself beyond her name, and the fact that she's a good kid."

"Her name's Violet?" Bexley's pulse throbbed against her neck. Surely there were dozens of teenage girls named after flowers. "How old?"

Grayson laid his forearms on the top of his car and let out a deep breath as he thought it over. "Well, she graduated from high school last spring and was accepted to PSC, so...I guess eighteen or nineteen."

Blood drained from Bexley's face. Could she have been talking with Lieutenant Baker's daughter the night before? The Violet that pledged with Kappa Kappa Delta seemed out of it, but more emotionally distraught than inebriated. Then again, it had been several hours since Bexley left the sorority house.

"Is she a platinum blonde with striking blue eyes?"

"That sounds accurate." Grayson tilted his head. "What's with the questions? Do you know her?"

"Come back inside." Swallowing past the lump in her throat, she set the gun on the railing. "We need to talk."

CHAPTER SEVEN

Grayson rubbed at his temples, groaning. "You're absolutely sure it was Violet?"

Bexley held up the girl's graduation invitation that Grayson had found in an office drawer full of pictures. "There's no question it was her."

His hard stare held hers. "And you're *positive* that she was alluding to the fact that there's hazing going on in that house?"

"I would bet my life on it, Grayson. She was really worked up over whatever they had done."

He popped up from his seat at the island, and began to pace the kitchen floor while fisting his hair. "The Lieutenant doesn't share a lot about his daughter with most people, but he would've told *me* if she was pledging with a sorority. I'm one of the only ones he trusts with that kind of thing."

"Those girls…you should've seen the way they lashed out when I confronted them about the collar. Violet was either tipsy or a little stoned when we talked, but she would've had to down an entire bottle of something to drink herself half to death. I'll bet they forced it on her after I left. I wouldn't be surprised if it was their way of punishing her for talking to me. We should check on Kayla Dahl—Temperance's dog handler. I wouldn't put it past them to do something to her, too."

"We can't simply storm into that sorority house and accuse them of hazing."

"*Why not?*" Bexley snarled. "If they did this to Violet, they need to be shut down!"

"You of all people know how this town works, Bex! Those girls are protected by parents with unlimited resources to make this kind of problem disappear!" Huffing out a short breath, he slipped back onto the stool beside her and gripped her knees. "If you're right about them forcing Violet to drink too much, the Lieutenant will have your back. But we won't know that for sure until she's awake. And before we go after them, we would need solid proof that would hold up in a court of law."

She placed her hands over his, appreciating the fact that he supported her theory without hesitation. He believed in her more than she believed in herself most days. "What if I can get Kayla to go on the record saying she was forced to steal the collar?"

"They'd simply deny it, and let her take the fall."

With an exasperated sound, she dropped her forehead against his shoulder. "I have to find a way to stop them before they hurt more girls."

"Let me and the lieutenant take care of it. They're not your responsibility."

"If my theory on what happened to Violet is right, then she's in the hospital because of *me*. I can't walk away knowing that."

One of his hands began to massage the back of her head. "Are you ready to talk about why you've been so jumpy lately?"

"Do I have to?" she muttered, leaning into his touch.

"You shot my garage door motor."

"I mean you really *could* use a new one."

"*Bexley.*"

"I guess I'm still...*processing* what happened

between me and Dean." It wasn't a total fib, but she wasn't in the mood to delve into the truth.

"I hate that your job will always put you in dangerous situations."

She leaned back with a choked laugh. "I could say the same about *your* job, Rivers."

His phone began to ring from inside his jacket, and he forced out a deep breath. "That's probably Lieutenant Baker, wondering what's taking so long. I'll bring him up to speed, and try my best to keep you updated. In the meantime, stay away from those girls, Bex. I mean it. You'll only get yourself in too deep to get back out." He stood and pressed his lips to the top of her head. "Maybe we can still grab a flight outta here by the end of the day."

***

WHILE GRAYSON HEADED into the station to fill his Lieutenant in on what Bexley had learned, she swung by Stronghold Investigations. As she raised her hand to knock on J.J.'s door, she heard him wheezing amidst a coughing fit, and pushed her way inside.

"Are you alright?" she asked, despite the obvious fact that he couldn't catch his breath. She knew enough about first aid to let him hack it out, as his lungs were at least getting enough air to release noise. But the godawful sounds were enough that she wondered if she should take him to the hospital. The coughing wasn't anything new since he'd smoked a tobacco pipe for decades, but it had become more prevalent in past months.

Once he finally stopped, he swiped a finger along the corner of each eye and smiled. "It's nothin' serious. Just couldn't catch my breath is all."

With a shake of her head, Bexley snorted. "What constitutes serious? Hacking up an actual lung? You should really see a doctor."

"Got me a physical scheduled in a couple'a weeks. I'll be alright until then." He gave her a stern look. "Shouldn't you be on a plane about now?"

"Our rendezvous to paradise has officially been post-phoned, thanks to the Papaya Springs PD." Lips pinched together, she plopped down in the ratty chair across from him. "I'm in a bit of a bind with a PSC sorority—Kappa Kappa Delta. Temperance's dog handler is rushing with them, and they all but admitted to my face that she took the collar as a part of hazing. But there's a more urgent problem that's come up involving one of their pledges that I spoke with late last night. A few hours after she told me there's something off about the sorority, she ended up in a coma with alcohol poisoning. I'm convinced she's there because the girls in her sorority were afraid she'd tell me their secrets. I know I'm not being paid to go after them, but it isn't sitting well with me. I feel like it's my moral obligation to investigate the situation further…especially when it might be my fault she's in this situation."

"Can't say I disagree. What do you need from me?"

"I was hoping for your blessing. Everything I do is linked back to this agency's reputation, and your standing in the community. I don't want to do anything to tarnish it."

Leaning back in his chair, he let out a deep chuckle. "Sweetheart, that ship sailed back in ninety-three when I called out a group of commissioners for embezzlin' taxpayer's money. You're not the only pariah in Papaya Springs. Why do you think I was so excited to bring you on board?"

A grin cracked her lips. "I figured it was because of my quick wit and charming people-skills."

His white eyebrows rose. "You have *my blessing* to

do whatever's necessary to bring down those spoiled-rotten girls."

She figured he'd back her up on this one, but his words still made her smile a little. "I wish Grayson was as understanding. He told me to leave it alone."

"Can't blame the boy for wantin' to keep you out of harm's way." J.J. tilted his head as his eyes narrowed with a confused glance. "He's a cop, darlin'. You knew that comin' into this. It's in his blood to protect, and he cares about you…pretty deeply, I might add. When he came to me askin' about the tickets, he mentioned it'd be good for you to spend a little time away with your family. I get the sense this weekend trip he arranged had less to do with leis and luaus, and more about what's coming next between the two of you."

A pang of stress beat against Bexley's temple. If J.J. was right, it could be the reason Grayson was pushing so hard for her to spend time with his parents. "Please don't tell me you mean marriage."

"And what'd be wrong with that?"

"I'm not ready for that. With him, or with anyone." She sighed while twisting her brown hair into a knot above her head. "I know Grayson's a great guy, and there are days I wonder what he's doing wasting his time with me, but I can't deal with the way he's always smothering me and pushing for us to spend more time together. Maybe I'm just not built for this relationship business."

"You're right, he *is* a great guy." J. J. nodded thoughtfully, tapping his chin. "That's why you need to figure things out—decide what it is you want before you lose 'im. Grayson's not the type to dilly-dally around. He knows a good thing when he sees it, and his sights are set on you. Marriage isn't all bad, kiddo. You tend to only see the bad things workin' at a place like this."

"Oh yeah? Then why isn't there a ring on *your* finger?"

He shrugged. "Had me a wife once. Pricilla Mae." The old man's eyes shone with happiness. "She was a looker, and a helluva cook too. Met her when she was just twenty, and ready to take on the world. I was twenty-five, fresh out of the military, and in the process of gettin' this place up and runnin'. We both fell hard and fast, got hitched within six months of meetin'. We couldn't wait to start us a family. It was her dream to fill a house to the rafters with kids. She was six months along with our first one when she was hit by a truck while bicy-clin' to classes at the college. Both her and our son died on the spot. Haven't found room in my heart for anyone else, I guess."

Bexley's eyes burned with tears. As much as J.J. loved delving into Bexley's personal business, he never said much about his own. She had always assumed he was a lifelong bachelor without any children. "I'm sorry, J.J.," she whispered. "I had no idea."

"It's 'cause I don't like to dwell on the past much. Nothin' I can do to change it anyhow." He cleared the phlegm from his throat and sat up a little taller. "Anyhow, just thought you should know getting married to the right person isn't the end of the world."

She wasn't sure Grayson was "the right person," but she wasn't going to get into that with her employer. "I better get going."

J.J. nodded. "Be careful, darlin'. And take it easy on Grayson. The man loves you with his whole heart. Far as I can tell, you're both lucky to have each other."

Normally she hated people telling her what to do, but she closed the door quietly behind her.

As Bexley was parking outside of the Kappa Kappa Delta sorority house, an unknown number flashed across her cell phone. Against her better judgment, she turned the car off and answered. "Bexley Squires."

"Bexley? This is Kitty Rivers. Grayson's mother?"

Slapping a hand over her forehead, Bexley's eyes shot up to the SUV's ceiling. "Yes, of course. How are you, Mrs. Rivers?"

"Concerned, really." The woman's voice was pinched, as if her uptight personality also strained her vocal chords. Bexley had only interacted with the one-time state beauty queen a handful of times back in high school. She had once witnessed his mother berating him for spending time with Bexley instead of his girlfriend at the time, and a few weeks later his mother found them drinking a beer in his backyard and threatened to send Grayson to military camp. Bexley hadn't seen or spoken to the woman since. Grayson's second-hand stories of Kitty's fundraisers and elaborate shindigs in Napa Valley had been enough.

"Bexley, I find it peculiar that you and Grayson have been seeing each other for over half *a year*, and we have yet to be reacquainted. First it was the missed dinner that Grayson had worked so hard to prepare for us, now he's telling me you have to cancel on our plans for the weekend. Is there a reason you don't want to be around us? Have we done something to offend you?"

Bexley's fingernails dug into the steering wheel. What had Grayson said that made her think such a thing? "It's nothing against you and Mr. Rivers. I've been tied up at work—"

"Yes, which is *also* highly disconcerting. The kind of hours you're keeping are not appropriate for the future mother of my grandch—"

"Whoa!" Sweat prickled against her forehead with the thought of becoming pregnant. Is that the direction in which Grayson assumed their relationship was heading? Is that why he didn't approve of her working so hard? "If Grayson and I were to consider starting a *family* together—and for your information we *have not*—that would be private conversation between the two of us."

"I would certainly hope *your husband* would have a say in how often you worked."

Between J.J. and now Grayson's mother, Bexley had more than enough of the marriage talk. But if she didn't get her anger under control, she'd likely say something that would have her permanently banned from associating with the Rivers family for life. "I'm really sorry, Mrs. Rivers. I didn't mean any disrespect. You've caught me at a bad time. We had to cancel this weekend because your son and I are working on the same case, and things have gotten ugly. I'm about to confront the bad guys, so my head isn't exactly in the right place for this kind of conversation. I'll call you back later."

She hit the end button before Kitty had a chance to reply. The consequences of their conversation would undoubtedly bite her in the ass later. She only hoped she had a chance to speak with Grayson before his mother relayed her own version of how it had gone down.

Waltzing up the front steps of Kappa Kappa Delta in broad daylight felt bold, all things considered, but the cunning sorority was already one step ahead. The double doors to the house swung open, spewing a handful of girls in matching red KKΔ t-shirts. They were accompanied by none other than Mayor Hoffman, the recently elected ruler of Papaya Springs, and Karl Jenkins, the district attorney.

Not long after Bexley had testified in Dean Halliwell's case, the powerful duo had tried to bring her down with trumped-up charges of slander. She suspected it had more to do with retribution for their clubhouse buddies she had helped send away for drug possession and solicitation. Luckily Grayson knew a good defense attorney who had the charges thrown out before she had to step foot in another courtroom.

Alicia, the vengeful redhead she'd met the other night, pushed her way to the front of the group, arms crossed and hip cocked. The other girls took on a similar stance, all at once making the situation feel comical.

"Is this the part where you break out in a chore-ographed dance and sing about the struggles of sorority life?" Bexley asked, cracking a sly smirk.

"You're not welcome here," Alicia snarled.

"If you don't leave the premises immediately, we'll have you brought in on charges of harass-ment," DA Jenkins added.

"Sure you want to go there again?" Bexley asked him. She scanned the group of girls until she found Maci, then Kayla. "I came here to find out what happened to Violet Baker."

Alicia raised her chin. "We don't know anyone by that name."

"Sure you do. The pledge I was talking to just last night...you know, the first time you tried to intimidate me?" When everyone remained tight-lipped, Bexley shook her head and let out a humorless laugh. "You can pretend all you want that this sorority had nothing to do with her trip to the hospital, but I'll expose the truth one way or another."

"You'd be wise to watch your back," Mayor Hoffman spat.

Bexley's lips curled with a smirk. "That'd be a great slogan for your upcoming campaign."

CHAPTER EIGHT

exley returned to the office to find J.J. in a meeting with a client. It was for the best since she wasn't looking forward to regurgitating the utter failure that included threats from some of the city's most influential leaders. She'd have to reorganize her thoughts, and find another way to catch the sorority red-handed.

Once she dived into less pressing cases an ongoing child support battle involving a wealthy realtor, and an investigation into an internet date that had gone so well that the client was sure there was something seriously wrong with the guy—the hours flew by. With a start, she realized it had almost been an entire business day since she last spoke with Grayson.

"Any news on Violet?" she asked as soon as he answered his cell.

"I wouldn't know. I've been tied up with *a judge and the DA* most of the afternoon."

Bexley's veins turned to ice. From the sharpness to his words, he sounded up to speed on Bexley's trip to Sorority Row.

"They've filed a restraining order keeping you away from Kappa Kappa Delta," he grumbled. "Damn it, Bex. You just couldn't stay away. Would it kill you to listen to me for a change?"

She was convinced it would. It wasn't in her nature to sit around and let problems resolve themselves. "I'm sorry. I wasn't trying to make your day more complicated."

He paused, letting out a sharp breath. "The sorority is denying any involvement with Violet. Same with her roommate in the dorms."

"Of course they are."

"We've run into a dead end. She hasn't used her debit card in over a week, and there isn't anything on her cell phone records that we can use. The lieutenant thinks she ditched the cell on their account since it hasn't moved out of her dorm room since she started classes."

"Does he think she would've rushed without telling him?"

"He wants to believe she wouldn't lie to her parents, but he also believes that you spoke to her last night." He let out another breath, sounding exhausted. "She's not doing so hot. The doctor told her family it's time to prepare for the worst outcome."

Regret burned behind Bexley's eyes. If the poor girl died, Bexley would never forgive herself for getting involved just enough to out Violet to the Deltas. "The Deltas are behind this, Grayson. If she doesn't make it, whoever forced the alcohol on her has to be held accountable. Please don't ask me to stay out of this matter again."

Grayson grunted into the phone. "We'll talk about it when I get home. The Lieutenant and his wife aren't coping too well with the situation, and I need to stick around in case whoever did this to Violet comes to pay her a visit. It'll be late. Don't wait up."

Bexley's lips parted with more to say, but he'd already ended the call.

A PERSISTENT BUZZ pulled Bexley from a light sleep. She hadn't remembered falling asleep while waiting for Grayson to return, but when she last checked the time, it was after midnight. She blindly snagged her phone from the nightstand and answered the call.

"Is this Bexley Squires?" a girly voice asked.

Bexley was beginning to think her number was scrawled on every bathroom stall in SoCal. She glanced over to where Grayson was asleep at her side, then quietly slid from the bed and crept into the hallway. "Who is this?" she whispered.

"It's Kayla Dahl. I've been thinking about what you said…that Temperance deserves to be happy after the thing with Dean. She's been, like, really nice to me, and I don't want her to suffer any longer. If I return the collar to you, how do I know you won't turn me into the cops?"

"Because I don't work for law enforcement. And I'll leave the decision up to you on whether or not to tell Temperance you're the one who took it. I just want to return it to her so she can go on with her life and begin to heal. I think you want the same thing."

"Meet me in the parking lot of PSC conservatory on the south side of campus in one hour. If you don't come alone, the deal's off. And don't even think about telling that detective boyfriend of yours where you're going."

She hated that the girl knew about Grayson, but it wasn't exactly a surprise since the Mayor and DA had become involved. "You're doing the right thing, Kayla. I'm on my way."

<hr>

THE COLLEGE'S elaborate conservatory quickly made Bexley's list of places never to venture in the dark while alone and dealing with possible assassins. At three in the morning, eerie shadows were cast by the glass building in all shapes and sizes, giving Bexley the impression that she wasn't alone. Every little movement she made, every quivering breath was met with an answering sound from somewhere in the depths of the shallow cluster of trees nearby. She wrapped her fingers around her stun gun in her handbag, ready to zap any threat that spewed out of the dark.

Minutes after she was to meet with Kayla, a meaty hand clamped around Bexley's nose and mouth. Her heart squeezed, but she was ready. She swung the stun gun through the air, aimed at her attacker.

The hands of a second person at her side snaked around her wrist and squeezed her arm.

The electric charge electrified in the darkness before her hand was forced to release the weapon. It clattered at her feet.

The person behind Bexley wrapped their second arm tightly around her belly.

Bexley's body numbed with a paralyzing fear.

She was trapped.

Completely helpless.

"You're a feisty one," a deep woman's voice rasped in her ear. The sickly odor of sweat wafted through the air. "Do everything we say, and you'll walk away in one piece. Nod if you understand."

Regaining control of her fitful breaths, Bexley fixed her eyes on the dark figures that appeared before her eyes when she obediently bobbed her head. These were college girls whose biggest aspirations involved throwing the best parties on campus and inventing new ways to deplete daddy's money in the process. She'd taken her determination to stop them a step too far, and they were merely sending the message that her meddling wasn't welcomed.

So they wanted to play a game? Bexley thought. *Batter up.*

Her handbag was yanked from her shoulder and dumped onto the pavement. A small, feminine figure wearing black leggings and a black hoodie knelt over the contents with her back to Bexley. She produced Bexley's cellphone, and another figure dressed in all black snagged it from the girl's hand before promptly stomping the screen with the heel of a boot. Then the girl rummaging through Bexley's things found her gun.

"Wouldn't you know, the bitch came packing," a man sniggered from somewhere in the dark. Bexley tried best as she could to memorize the lilt of the man's voice.

Had the Mayor or DA joined the girls to ensure Bexley was properly warned?

Her spirits plummeted as the gun was handed off to another hooded figure. They'd not only rendered her defenseless, but could easily take her out with her own weapon. She suddenly wished she had told Grayson about the shooting, or even that she had woken him before heading out to meet Kayla. Maybe he was right to be worried about her. She had a knack for finding danger, but lacked the smarts to find her own way out.

Small, soft hands gathered Bexley's arms behind her back. Seconds after they were bound with handcuffs, she was released by the Emma Stone impersonator, and a satiny bag was slipped over her head. Before she could release the breath she had been holding, she was nudged back into a set of waiting arms. Someone simultaneously lifted her legs. For a group of young adults, they certainly had their kidnapping skills honed to a degree that would make a serial killer envious.

"This isn't necessary," she announced to her unseen captors. "I already gave Kayla my word that no one would go to jail. And did you really have to do that to my phone? I almost had it paid off. It's not like I was gonna snap all my friends the details of what went down here tonight."

"You were right," another man's voice grumbled above her. "She never shuts up."

The hands unceremoniously dropped her, and she fell several feet onto something hard. As she was trying to catch her breath from the harsh impact, the sound of a door slamming inches away cut off the cool evening air. She was trapped. In a trunk.

Her airway tightened as an engine roared to life. Her head slid into the side of the trunk as the vehicle jerked into drive. Something that desperately wanted to be identified as music blasted above her head. Then a voice began to scream along with the aggressive guitar riffs. *Hey, I know that voice,* Bexley thought. Though the obnoxious decibel could've very likely ruptured an eardrum, she thrashed her head along to the beat for a moment. It would take far more than a little Marilyn Manson to rattle her cage. He had been Cineste's artist of choice while going through a rebellious phase against the Captain, and it had done a fair job of testing his limits.

Before long, her hot breaths warmed the satin bag over her head to a stifling degree. Her bladder pulsated, threatening to let go. *They're just kids trying to give you a good scare,* she reminded herself once again. But a nagging sensation told her otherwise. A second man's voice was the last thing she heard before they'd imprisoned her in the trunk. Neither of the men's voices sounded familiar. Maybe they had hired thugs to get the job done.

She blindly pivoted around on her back, getting a feel for her surroundings with the tip of her tennis shoe. Once she was sure she had found the area where the tail lights should be, she kicked with all her might. But her foot was met with resistance.

Her kidnappers had thought ahead and reinforced her prison.

It was impossible to track the vehicle's movements. She suspected they were driving like maniacs for the sole purpose of confusing her, and they were doing a stellar job. Her thoughts were so consumed by her fate and keeping her shorts dry that she had no concept of time once the vehicle came to a complete stop. Had she been in there for minutes? Hours?

The trunk door whooshed open above her. The distinct sound of rushing water was a reminder of how close she had come to wetting herself in the trunk. She was carried out from the trunk in a set of a man's thick arms. His sandalwood scent was too clean and far too expensive to belong to a thug. She couldn't get a sense of him otherwise as she was carried up a few steps, then down a long stairway into a cool and damp room that was thick with a musty odor.

The notion that she might not make it out alive was becoming an unsettling reality. Grayson had saved her from Dean Halliwell's wrath by tracking her cell phone. There was no chance of that happening this time around.

She was deposited onto a wooden chair, and her

cuffed hands crushed against one of its rails. Yelping, she leaned forward to move her hands. At the same time, something sharp stabbed deep into her left thigh muscle.

"What *the hell* was that?" she cried out, panting heavily into the bag still over her face.

"Something to help you relax," a digitized voice answered.

The soft bag was yanked from her head, sending strands of her hair falling around her face. Her eyes slowly adjusted through her locks to a dimly lit room. She was surrounded by a handful of women wearing the kind of grotesque animal masks featured in modern-day horror films. Two tall, husky men in black shirts and pants with similar masks stood behind them like statues. *More like bodyguards, or hitmen,* Bexley mused with a shudder.

"I get it now. The voice changer…the tacky masks…someone in this room is a diehard *Scream* fan. Before you bother asking for my favorite scary movie, you should know that I don't scare that way, because I have a strong sense of fiction versus reality. In real life, the bad guys always lose and end up behind bars."

One of the beefy men stepped forward, striking her cheekbone with the back of his hulking hand.

Bexley roared. Pain exploded behind her eyeball and through her jaw. For a moment she wondered if her eye had been knocked out of its socket entirely.

"What part of this makes you think we're messing around?" the man asked, his features hidden beneath a malformed hog mask. "This is no joke."

"Can't help it. I'm deflecting. My therapist says I'm a lost cause." Bexley flexed her jaw several times, attempting to assess whether or not any teeth were missing. "But someone needs to be accountable for the reason why Violet Baker's in a coma."

"Do you have any idea how many people in Papaya Springs would pay good money to have you silenced?" The man crossed his thick arms over his bulging pectoral muscles. "If you were smart, you would've gone back to New York when you had the chance."

Bexley all at once felt floaty. The man's voice and image became distorted. She squeezed her eyes closed for a moment, and the muscles in her eyelids jerked. What had they injected into her thigh?

"I get it," she told the man. "You don't like me."

"No, you don't get it," the digitized voice answered. "Everyone in this room *despises* you. And we've decided it's past time you learn a valuable lesson."

An unmasked girl with a dirty blond balayage rushed at Bexley. The girl's image flicked in and out like a broken television. Her features were too distorted to register.

Bexley wasn't entirely convinced she wasn't dreaming.

The flicker of a large blade in the girl's hands caught in the dim light.

THE WORLD WAS A BLUR.

Bexley's bare feet stumbled across gravel.

The warm glow of daylight breached her surroundings. She was on the side of a quiet highway. Confusion gripped her memories.

Where exactly was she?

How did she get there?

She remembered a dark basement and someone wanting to hurt her. When she tried remembering the specifics, she was only able to recall a bunch of weirdness in general.

Her attention shifted to flashing lights off in the distance.

Men in tan uniforms beside sheriff cars barricaded the road ahead.

Brass, angry voices warbled against her eardrums, sounding as if they were coming from the other side of a long tunnel.

"Don't move!"

"Drop the weapon!"

"Get on your knees!"

The sounds and lights were making her dizzy. Her spotty vision traveled downward ever so slowly as she lowered her chin.

Every movement she made was jerky, like she was stuck in a psychedelic music video.

She felt broken, as if she had lost all control of her body.

Her heart thudded at a snail's pace.

She was numb from head to toe.

What was happening?

It felt as if she was floating above herself when she noticed something red splattered across her gray tank top and white running shorts.

Was that blood?

Was it hers?

"Hold on!" a man called out. "I know her! She's Detective Rivers's girlfriend! Lower your weapons!"

There was a pause, then, *"I said lower your goddamn weapons! It's Bexley Squires!"*

She jumped when a baby-faced officer appeared directly in front of her, empty hands held up. Every time she blinked, he moved in a disjointed manner. Almost like a puppet on strings. Why did everything look so odd?

"Bexley?" the man asked. His eyes traveled down to her hands. "Oh my god, Bexley. What have you done?"

She looked down to her right hand.

A knife.

The sharp, serrated tip covered in…*was that blood too?*

Vomit thickened in her throat.

What *had* she done?

PART II

CHAPTER NINE

PAPAYA SPRINGS, CALIFORNIA

AUGUST 12TH

Kayla Dahl's stomach twisted painfully hard as she gazed across the street to the ostentatious houses that made up Sorority Row. Hundreds of girls her age traveled in packs from mansion to mansion, bubbling with energy and enlivened conversation as they followed their group leader around like ducklings. Kayla had stressed for weeks on what style of dress to buy and how to do her hair, hoping she wouldn't stand out as a transplant. Back home, she'd been one of the most popular girls at her small school. In this strange town where the rich kids were treated like celebrities, she was starting to feel like a nobody.

Her mom had told her stories of rush, and Kayla had done enough research to know what to expect, but she hadn't been excited by the idea of pledging from the start. Her mom had pledged with Kappa Kappa Delta, and she expected her only daughter to follow in her footsteps. For that same reason, Kayla had applied to her mom's alma mater in California rather than going to a state school or the University of Minnesota like most of her friends. The girls she'd met in California had given her a chilly reception from day one. The idea of pitching herself to a room full of them was terrifying.

"Are you hoping to pledge with Kappa Kappa Delta too?" a singsong voice asked at her side.

Kayla looked up to discover their group had arrived at their first destination. She'd been so anxious that she hadn't been paying attention to where her feet were taking her. The stately home made of brick and stone loomed above her with a baleful vibe, and the Greek letters hung above the door almost took her breath away. A large cluster of girls gathered on the steps, waiting for the open house to begin. She was no longer sure she was prepared for what was to come.

"I think so," she muttered. "I'm super nervous."

"I think it's safe to say that everyone here is to some degree. Some of them are just better at hiding it." The girl at her side was a gracefully tall blonde with a friendly smile and a petite little nose. The way her pearly white teeth sparkled in the California sun and her platinum hair flowed over her narrow shoulders like strands of silk reminded Kayla of a surfer she'd seen in a commercial on TV, inviting visitors to their sunny state. Her white sundress was remarkably similar to Kayla's with an empire waist and wide straps, and their hair was curled in the same beach waves. She offered Kayla a slender hand with bubble gum pink nails. "I'm Violet."

"Kayla."

As they shook hands, Kayla was relieved when she caught a whiff of violet-scented perfume. Knowing she would have to remember so many names that week had given her a stomach ache, but this girl's would be hard to forget.

Violet's lips spread with a mischievous grin. "What do you say we go in there and stir shit up, Kayla?"

Giggling, they locked arms and headed toward the double doors.

AFTER THE OPEN house was over, Kayla and Violet found a late night ice cream shoppe right across the street from campus. Other hopeful recruits filled a few tables, but a majority of the tables were packed with boisterous drunks.

The two new friends shared a hot fudge sundae the size of a football while summarizing the experience of meeting the sororities. Kayla thought it was intense and highly overwhelming. But with Violet at her side, her anxieties had melted before they'd even stepped inside the first house.

"We deserve this after tonight," Violet decided, digging her spoon into the gooey treat. "My face hurts from the fake smile plastered on my lips. I swear I'll still be smiling after I go to sleep."

Kayla giggled. "My stomach hurts from all the times you made me laugh!"

Violet shoved the spoonful into her mouth and shrugged. "Can't help it. Some of those girls were begging to be mocked." She waved the spoon through the air like a princess. "Oh, hello, minion…my daddy is uber rich and paid my way into this college. Do you like my five carat diamond earrings? They're so tacky, but my ten carat earrings are being cleaned."

Ice cream splattered from Kayla's lips when she cackled. "Oh my god, that's spot on!"

"Like who are these rich bitches, anyway? They act like their families own the state of California."

A wave of excitement hit Kayla. "Wait. You don't come from a rich family either?"

"Not exactly." Violet lifted one shoulder while taking another bite of the frozen desert. "I mean my parents make a decent amount, just not to Kappa Kappa Delta standards. But don't worry, it's not like they can look into your bank account or anything. Just act like you're one of them, and they won't question it. You're probably in since your mom was a Delta anyway. My parents don't even know I'm rushing."

Kayla's shoulders drooped. Her grandparents were wealthy, and her mom had gotten in without scholarships, but Kayla didn't know there was a socioeconomic requirement to become a Delta. If it weren't for her top-notch grades, her parents wouldn't have been able to afford to send her to California.

"Can we discuss the door stack thing now?" Violet asked.

Kayla briefly covered her eyes with one hand. "Oh my god, that was the worst! I'm gonna have nightmares for life after that!"

Violet's sky-blue eyes rolled to the fluorescent lights over their heads. "I think they may've actually been trying to summon demons with that business."

Smiling at her new friend, Kayla reached out to touch her arm. "I'm sooooo glad we met. I'm not sure I would've made it through all of this without you."

"Ditto." Laughing, Violet twisted her arm so she was holding Kayla's as well. "Promise me we'll stick together, no matter what happens, and watch each other's backs. I've heard sorority life can get… brutal."

Unease pressed against Kayla's shoulders as she nodded. Her mom hadn't mentioned anything that could be described as "brutal." What was she getting herself into? "Of course. I get the feeling we'll be friends for life."

CHAPTER TEN

Violet and Kayla survived the house tours and philanthropy rounds. Before they knew it, the final phase of rush week had arrived. In her grandmother's pearls and a navy dress detailed in lace that she'd worn to her cousin's wedding dress rehearsal, Kayla tackled the pref night party like a pro. She proved to the Kappa Kappa Deltas that she belonged, especially when approached by the sorority's president.

Alicia Stryker was a stunning redhead, luscious long locks and sharp features of her face made up like she was on her way to a photoshoot. "You're the one who works for Temperance Rose, right?" she asked Kayla in a sugary sweet tone. "Isn't her dog worth, like, a million dollars?"

Kayla shrugged. "I don't know about that, but people pay a lot of money for the Samoyed breed."

"Does she let you take the dogs on walks and whatever by yourself?"

Warning bells rang through Kayla's head. "Yeah…sure."

Glancing back at a group of Kappa Kappa Delta sisters watching them, Alicia tapped her chin before throwing Kayla a devious smile. "I think I may know a sure way for you to get a bid."

WHEN BID DAY ARRIVED, both Violet and Kayla were invited to join Kappa Kappa Delta. The bid came as a relief to Kayla once she was able to call her mom with the news. The house celebrated that night by roller skating, and allowing the new pledges to mingle.

Their first official day as Deltas, the big sisters ordered the pledges to do little things as they followed them around campus. First they were instructed to carry a marble on their person at all times. They'd even checked on the pledges when using the bathroom. Then the very next day, they were told to also wear ribbons in the Kappa Kappa Delta colors. Violet and Kayla found the traditions strange, and even laughed about it that night while lying in their beds.

The next day, their other roommate, Sarah—a new pledge from San Diego—was caught at the gym without her ribbons. Rumor spread quickly that they had forced Sarah into a car, and no one had seen or heard from her in hours. She was the most mild-mannered of the new pledges, and not the type to purposely break any rules.

That night, as Kayla and Violet stared at the ceiling from their beds, Kayla was worried sick about Sarah's fate. The sorority's bedrooms were massive enough to accommodate three double beds and still have enough room for their desks and some lounging chairs, but it was beginning to feel like a prison cell. With every day that passed, she felt a little more restricted.

"Do you think they kicked her out?" Kayla asked.

Violet snorted, sounding way less concerned. "I doubt it. All her stuff is still here. They're probably just trying to scare the rest of us so we don't stray from the rules…even if they are still incredibly dumb."

"Better not let them hear you say that!" Kayla hissed.

Violet boldly laughed. "I'm not scared of them. There's only so much they can do to us."

They soon fell asleep, but woke just before midnight when a shadowed figure moved across their room, accompanied by sniffling.

"Sarah?" Violet called out. She reached out to turn the lamp on between their beds. "Are you alright?"

Drops of water fell from Sarah's chestnut brown hair and sky blue t-shirt, pooling on the hardwood floor. She was soaked to the bone. As she stared back at her roommates, her teeth chattered together.

"Oh my god!" Kayla jumped from bed with her comforter in hand, and threw it over Sarah's shoulders. "What happened?"

Sarah held the blanket tight around her chin. "Alicia and the others…they t-took me shopping… made me buy a ch-charm bracelet from T-tiffany's with my emergency c-credit card."

"Oookay." Violet side-eyed Kayla as she stood to rub their roommate's shoulders. "That's harmless enough. We'll help you take it back tomorrow."

"They t-took me to the ocean," Sarah contin-ued. "They made me t-throw it in!"

Violet clicked her tongue. "What? You can't be serious."

Sarah's big blue eyes filled with tears. "I t-tried to find it…thought maybe it'd w-wash back to s-shore. My d-dad's gonna kill me!"

"This is bullshit!" Violet seethed, fisting her hands at her sides.

"Shhh," Kayla scolded, holding a finger to her lips. "Seriously, Violet! You're gonna get all of us kicked out if you don't be quiet!"

"Doesn't matter! They can't do this to her!" Violet motioned to their roommate. "What's she supposed to tell her dad?"

Shaking her head, Kayla put a hand on Sarah's shoulder. She felt sympathetic for her new friend, especially because if Kayla had been in her shoes, their parents probably would've made her move back to Minnesota. But if this was how the Kappa Kappa Deltas wanted you to play along, she wasn't going to create any waves. "No offense, Sarah, but your dad owns a helicopter and a private jet. Do you really think he's going to freak about a stupid bracelet?"

"It's the principle of it all that matters!" Violet

argued, stepping between them. "Everyone else here is rich. *We get it.* No need to act like assholes with money to get a point across! Why did they invite us to join? So they could rub their wealth in our faces?"

There was a brisk knock on their door before it flung open. Alicia Stryker, the Delta's president, stood in a bubblegum pink shorts and tank top set, fiery red hair recently brushed, thin hands on her delicate hips. Her emerald green eyes fell directly on Violet. "Is there a problem in here?"

Violet responded with a tense smile. "Just trying to warm her up before she gets pneumonia."

"I hope *everyone* learned a valuable lesson today," Alicia said, responding with her own sickly sweet smile. "Do as you're told, and things will go smoothly. But if you mess with us, we'll make your life a living hell."

CHAPTER ELEVEN

In the day that followed the bracelet incident, the pledges were sure to do everything they were told without hesitation. The lightheartedness that came with rush week was long gone by the time nightfall came, and they were all ushered into the basement like cattle. The older sisters clustered in front of them like a wild pack of dogs on the verge of attack. Tension thickened the air.

Alicia stood in front, arms folded over her KKΔ t-shirt. "Some of us feel you ladies aren't taking the sisterhood seriously."

Kayla's pulse quickened. Was this because of what had happened in their room the night before? She tried to make eye contact with Violet, but her friend's stone-cold gaze was locked with Alicia's.

Neither seemed ready to back down from the silent challenge.

"Each and every one of you pledges are to find a place to stand facing these walls," Alicia ordered with a crooked smile. "I want to see the tips of your imperfect little noses making contact with the brick." When everyone seemed too afraid to move, her smile turned into a sneer and she screamed, *"Now,* dammit!"

The pledges scattered. Violet and Kayla settled in next to each other.

"Promise me you'll do everything she says," Kayla pleaded in a whisper.

Violet didn't answer. Her jaw flexed as she stared at the wall.

Alicia paced back and forth behind them. "If you move from this position, you will be reprimanded. I don't care if your nose itches, or you feel a cough coming, or you have to piss yourself. You will *not* move even a mere millimeter until I say."

"Are you kidding?" Violet muttered.

"What was that?" Alicia snapped, marching in their direction.

"How exactly is this supposed to prove our loyalty?" Violet asked.

"By proving that you'd do anything for your sisters, no

matter the situation!" From the tension and anger in Alicia's tone, it sounded as if she was one heartbeat away from throwing a complete fit. *"Are we going to have a problem?"*

Violet grumbled something in response. Kayla's heart lurched with the flurry of movement she caught from the corner of her eye. There was a sickening thud, like the sound of a hand slapping against pavement, then a yelp from Violet and several gasps.

Kayla couldn't stop herself from turning to look. Violet was holding a hand over her face, and blood covered her fingers. Tears clogged Kayla's throat when she realized Alicia had slammed Violet's face into the brick.

"Get a good look while you can, ladies," Alicia sang, "because this is what's going to happen to the next one of you who thinks they're too good to follow my orders! Now stick those damn noses against the pavement and don't you dare move a muscle! That means you too, Violet!"

Kayla rested a hand on her friend's arm. "But she's bleeding!"

Alicia shrugged. "It's a superficial wound—not like she's going to bleed out. Now put your damn nose up against the wall before you have an accident too!"

Kayla's eyes flashed between Alicia and Violet. "But—"

"Just do it, Kayla," Violet snarled, removing her hand from her face to face the wall. Kayla saw the bits of skin missing from Violet's nose and cheeks, like the kind of scratches one would get from falling off a bike.

ONCE THEY WERE ALLOWED to leave the basement several hours later, Violet stormed past everyone toward their room. When Kayla caught up with her, Violet was frantically shoving her clothes into her suitcase.

Kayla froze in the doorway. "Where are you going?"

"I'm leaving," Violet announced, sniffling. "What they're doing to us isn't right. Not only because it's illegal, but it's disgusting! We're supposed to be their new sisters! Who *does* that to someone they consider to be a future friend? They're mentally whacked in this place, Kayla!"

"Keep your voice down. They'll hear you."

Violet spun around with tears spilling from her beautiful blue eyes and pooling into the fresh blood on her face. "I don't care what those bitches think of me! I can't do this anymore! Come with me, Kayla! Let's get outta here before it gets worse!"

Kayla knew Violet was right. Alicia had taken things too far. But the clever president had ensured Kayla would take the sisterhood more seriously than the others. "I can't leave. There's something I have to tell you." Her shoulders rolled forward, and she sighed. "Your nose…it's still bleeding. I'll tell you everything while we get you cleaned up."

CHAPTER TWELVE

Hours after she'd told Violet her story and convinced her to stay, Kayla laid wide awake, listening to the steady breathing of her roommates. She was still traumatized by what Alicia had done to Violet, and wanted to sneak out into the hallway to call her mom. She'd know what to do, and how to fix the mess Kayla had gotten into. It'd even be worth the disappointment she'd see in her mother's eyes. But truth was, Kayla was more afraid of the consequences once Alicia discovered Kayla had snitched.

Still dehydrated from standing in the dry basement for so long, she snuck down to the kitchen for a glass of water. She didn't want to risk the chance of running into Alicia. The kitchen was mostly quiet, except for the hum of the industrial appliances, and the faint murmur of a TV and giggles in the gathering room down the hallway. She nearly dropped the glass in her hand when she heard someone whisper her name.

Violet padded barefoot to her side. "Sorry I scared you. I couldn't sleep."

"Me either." Noticing the scabs beginning to form on her friend's face, Kayla let out a shaky sigh. "Are you alright?"

"I'll live." Violet steered around her to grab a glass from the cabinet. "I can't stop thinking about that dog collar."

Kayla's heart sank. "I wish I would've said something to you about it sooner. I don't know what I was thinking when I agreed to Alicia's idea. It's just…my mom is making such a big deal about this place. I guess I didn't want to let her down, and I was eager to impress Alicia."

"I get it, but you should really return the collar. If it's worth as much as they're saying, you could do serious time. Do you really want to start a career with a felony on your record?"

"Alicia threatened to tell the cops," Kayla told her, shaking her head. "You know she'd deny everything if I told Temperance what happened."

"So let's find out where they're keeping it, and you can sneak it back into Temperance's house. She doesn't have to know you're the one who took it."

"Alicia would find out," Kayla insisted with fear squeezing her heart. "I just know it!"

Just then, they heard the front door slam shut, and a girl scream, *"You little bitch!"*

Violet set her glass down and snagged Kayla's hand, leading her down the hallway. They peered around the corner of the gathering room, finding the older sisters cuddled on the couches. A dirty blonde loomed over them, body tense and coiled as if ready to throw punches.

Alicia appeared neither afraid nor amused the way she rolled her eyes at the girl, palm of her hand held upward. "Stop right there, psycho. This isn't the time nor the place for one of your rants."

"What did you tell Dad?" the blonde demanded, not backing down. "He put a hold on my bank account! Why does he think I dropped out of school?"

Glancing at the other sisters on the couch, Alicia twisted a red lock around her finger and rolled her eyes. "Um, maybe because you *did?*" The sisters giggled wickedly.

"What I do is none of your damn business!" the

blonde roared. *"I was going to tell him once I figured out what I'm going to do next!"*

Rising from the couch, Alicia crossed her arms under her chest. "This is exactly why you could never be a Delta, *Dayna*. Sometimes I can't believe we share the same DNA. You're incapable of showing loyalty to anything or anyone. Why do you think Daddy hates you so much? He knows you're hopeless! You're always doing things just to piss him off!"

"And now he knows you're a total slut!" Dayna fired back. She mirrored Alicia's pose, and grinned proudly. "I told him that you have chlamydia!"

Color drained from Alicia's face. "How would you know?"

Dayna tipped her chin the direction of the couch. "One of your *loyal* Delta sisters told me."

"What?" Alicia shrieked, spinning around to the other Deltas. "Which one of you blabbed?"

Violet released a loud snort. Belatedly, she slapped her hands over her mouth.

But it was too late. Alicia's bitter green eyes were already glaring their way.

CHAPTER THIRTEEN

Darkness surrounded Kayla, pulsating like a living thing. Brash guitar riffs blasted from a speaker behind her head along with a man's baritone voice shrieking incomprehensible lyrics. The stale air around her felt limited. With every gulping breath, she feared it'd be her last. Her body painfully thrashed against the trunk's hard floor with every bump in the road. She was more terrified than she'd ever been. The only thing keeping her from crying hysterically was Violet's hand, tightly bound around her own. Trying to communicate over the blaring music would be useless, but knowing her new friend was close and experiencing the same nightmare gave her comfort.

After what felt like hours, the vehicle slammed

to a standstill. The engine was cut, but the screaming music remained as the door creaked over them. Kayla's teeth began to chatter. What was Alicia planning to do to them? She was so angry when she caught them listening in on her conversation with her sister that she was literally trembling from head to toe.

Kayla was terrified—even more so than the time a misbehaved German Shepard bit off one of her fingers and she had to hold it on the way to the hospital.

"On your feet!" Alicia roared.

Kayla waved her hands around, trying to find the edge of the trunk. A hand gripped her forearm, dragging her over the metal lip and scraping skin off her thigh. Warm summer air whooshed around her as she fell, quickly catching herself with her hands on soft ground before she face-planted. Over the sound of rushing water nearby, she heard the soft *oomph* of Violet falling beside her.

"I said, on your feet, bitches! Are you deaf?"

"Don't let her break you," Violet whispered in Kayla's ear. "We'll get through this together."

The two girls located each other's fumbling hands, and helped each other to stand. Then the blindfolds were yanked from their heads. A blinding light shone back and forth into their eyes. Wincing loudly, they covered their faces with their hands.

"You two think you're pretty clever, don't you?" Alicia snarled, shining the light on Kayla. "I suppose you were planning on telling the other pledges everything you heard!"

"No way," Kayla answered with tears streaming down her face. "We would never do that."

The light flickered to Violet's face. "What about you?"

Violet's lips spread into a tight line.

"Your loyalty has remained questionable from day one," Alicia said. "It's time you prove yourself once and for all." She motioned to Maci who stood at her side. "Put it on her."

Maci, the sorority's vice president and Alicia's loyal guard dog, approached Violet. Cinderella's collar sparkled in the light.

All at once, Kayla couldn't breathe. "What are you going to do with that?" she demanded.

"I'm going to teach your little friend a lesson," Alicia answered. Once the collar was secure around Violet's neck, Alicia lifted her phone. "Now smile like you mean it."

Violet looked back at her with an empty expression.

"If you don't put on a happy face, I'm calling the cops right this minute and telling them you both broke into Temperance Rose's house and stole it!"

The smile Violet gave her looked more like a grimace, but it seemed to appease Alicia once she had taken a few pictures. "Disrespect me again or even *think* about abandoning your sisters, and I'll send these pictures to both Temperance and the cops."

Maci removed the collar, holding it as she rejoined Alicia.

"Now this is the part where you prove your allegiance to this sorority. Both of you get into the creek behind you."

Kayla and Violet exchanged a terrified look.

Alicia clicked her tongue and gave a harsh giggle. "It's not deep enough to drown in, you morons. Not unless you force me to put you in there and hold your heads down. You're merely going to do a little midnight workout."

Reluctant, the two girls turned to face the stream of water behind them. It was wider than Kayla had expected, and ran alongside a creepy abandoned house—the kind they use in horror movies. Between the house and creek, there was a deep bank of fresh mud. The idea of crawling into the dirty water in the darkness made Kayla's body numb with fear.

"Down on your hands and knees!" Alicia barked. "We're going to start with push-ups! Mess them up, and you'll get my foot in your back!"

Violet slowly turned around. "No."

With a cold cackle, Alicia reached one arm behind her. Her features were scrunched in anger, and her face was a deep shade of red. "You may want to reconsider your answer." Her hand snaked back around her hip, wielding a large, threatening gun. She pointed it directly at Violet.

"*Ali!*" Maci screamed, backing away from her friend. "What are you *doing?*"

"I'm done letting people think they can walk all over me!" Alicia cried.

Tears poured down Kayla's face. She tugged on Violet's t-shirt. "Get down and do what she says, V! *Please!*"

Holding Alicia's furious scowl, Violet refused to move. Before she knew what was happening, Alicia darted forward and struck her with the gun.

PART III

CHAPTER FOURTEEN

PAPAYA SPRINGS, CALIFORNIA

*S*creaming music.
Terrifying masks.
An angry girl.
She was trapped.

But Bexley couldn't recall anything that involved bloodshed. Her body didn't feel pain, or the telltale burn of an injury. Had she stabbed someone? Had she been attacked? The dark-haired kid with pretty green eyes standing before her looked familiar, but…

"Do you remember me? My name's Adam Danks. I helped Grayson take your sister to the hospital…before I became a sheriff's deputy."

"What's happen'ng?" she slurred. What was wrong with her voice? Why did it take so much effort to speak? "How'd I get h're?"

"I was hoping you could tell me. Are you hurt?"

"I don't thin' so." Her teeth clamped down through her garbled words. She was dizzy. She just wanted to lay down.

"Did you take something? Maybe a Valium?"

The slow burn of anger ignited in her gut. "No…no way."

"Okay, I believe you." The deputy's eyes fixated on her hands. "Could you do me a big favor and drop that knife? It's making the other deputies behind me uneasy. We're here to help you, but that won't happen if you're seen as a viable threat."

Her sporadic vision slowly skipped down to the knife again. The blade was extremely large, like something a hunter would use to skin an animal hide. Sickness swelled in her stomach. Where had it come from? Why was it covered in blood? Her hand jerked, tossing it on the ground. Her body quivered violently as her legs buckled.

Deputy Danks caught her in his arms. "Whoa! I've got you. Everything's going to be okay, Bexley. We'll figure this out." He glanced over his shoulder. "I could use some help here!"

Time skated past in the blink of an eye. Something heavy and warm was placed over her shoulders. She was nudged into a car.

"It's okay, Bexley," Deputy Danks told her. The outline of his skinny frame danced before her eyes. "Grayson will know what to do."

<hr>

INSIDE A STARK GRAY INTERROGATION ROOM, Bexley sat alone at a metal table, hunched over a cup of the most revolting black coffee she'd ever tasted. Although she only vaguely remembered taking a shower, her hair hung in damp clumps around her shoulders, and the crisp smell of generic soap stung her nostrils. She didn't remember being given the SHERIFF hoodie and sweatpants she wore, or the wool blanket draped over her shoulders. But she was grateful for their warmth as it effectively kept her never-ending chills at bay. Nausea lingered in the pit of her stomach. She was bruised, battered, and exhausted.

Most of all, her head hurt from trying to piece everything together. There was a gaping hole in her memory that began after she was taken into a basement, and ended around the time she was being examined by a doctor in the Emergency Room.

She knew she didn't have it in her to hurt an innocent girl. If she had truly stabbed someone, it would've been for a damn good reason. *Unless you were so high that you were paranoid and didn't understand what was happening at the time,* her conscience said. Still, she knew she didn't willingly ingest drugs.

"Why the hell didn't someone call me sooner?" Grayson's deep voice roared from the hallway.

"The sheriff wanted to keep her vulnerable—I snuck out as soon as I could," Deputy Danks answered, sounding equally annoyed. "She wasn't herself when we found her in the road. Her urine tested positive for ketamine, and they found a faint needle mark on her thigh. The doctor said she wouldn't remember anything that happened while she was under the influence of the drug."

"This is ridiculous!" Grayson barked back. "I'm taking her home!"

The heavy door to the room swung open, banging against the wall. Grayson rushed in, brown eyes intense. "Bex, thank God you're alright!" His arms locked around her, lifting her from the chair. He held onto her for a few ragged heartbeats, then lowered her back down, cupping her face in his hands. "Where'd you go? You scared the hell outta me!"

Her pulse skipped a little with the deeply embedded concern straining his tone. In a dry, cracked voice, she asked, "Still want to see me in that bikini, no matter where we spend the weekend?"

His expression instantly hardened. He stood and folded his arms over his chest. "All of this could've been avoided if you'd bother to fill me in on what you're doing for once. What were you thinking, going to meet those girls alone in the middle of the night? Honestly, I'm starting to think you have a death wish!"

"It was just supposed to be Kayla, and she sounded sincere. I didn't think—"

"That's exactly the problem you keep having!" he snarled. "You didn't think Halliwell would hurt you either!" He loomed over her like a dark cloud, scratching the stubble on his jaw. "You've managed to get yourself into one helluva mess this time!"

A band of anger tightened her chest as she pressed her lips into a tight line. He made her sound like some bumbling idiot in a comedy. Worst of all, it was the exact kind of thing her father would say.

What happened to Grayson's declaration of believing in her abilities?

"You don't recall anything that happened after you drove to the college? Do you remember where the knife came from, or how you got on that highway?"

Before she could answer, Sheriff Blair stomped into the room. He was a burly man in his early forties with a thick black mustache, dark hair beneath a cowboy hat trimmed to standard military length. Bexley had only met him once when he joined in on the search for Dean Halliwell's other victims, but the experience was enough to know he was unreasonable, bullheaded, and easily corrupt. Like the other residents of Papaya Springs, Bexley kept up-to-date on the man's questionable politics and sketchy agendas through the local news.

Tension crackled through the air as the sheriff eyed Grayson. The two men had butted heads several times during the investigation. Bexley suspected it was mostly due to the fact that unlike the sheriff, Grayson's efforts couldn't be diverted with a bribe. "Detective Rivers. Been awhile since I've seen you around."

Grayson's back stiffened. "Bexley's been through a lot. I came to bring her home."

"I'm afraid we need to have us a little chat with her before you can do that." The sheriff sniffled and swung a chair around to straddle it. "Dispatch received a call early this mornin' saying your *girlfriend* was involved in an altercation with a young woman who has since gone missing. The same young woman's car was discovered with a significant amount of blood in the interior, about a mile from the campus parking lot where we found Miss Squires's rental vehicle. The lab is processing the blood found on the knife against that in the victim's car to see if it's a match."

Nausea ripped through Bexley's esophagus. "Are you going to tell us this *young woman's* name, or is securing that kind of information beyond your skill set?"

The sheriff threw her a smug look. "Why don't *you* tell me her name, and we can be done playing this little game?"

"Without producing an actual victim, the DA's office doesn't have a leg to stand on," Grayson argued through gritted teeth. "You can't keep her here based on an anonymous call and a hunch."

"No matter." The sheriff leaned back in the chair, jamming his thumbs into his belt buckle. "I've sent my men out to comb the area near where the vehicle was found. One way or another, it won't be long until we have enough evidence to charge Miss Squires with something substantial."

With a persistent shake of his head, Grayson braced himself on the back of Bexley's chair. "This is bogus. For all you know, Bexley could've been a bystander to something brutal. She was *drugged*. Did you bother checking her for defensive wounds?"

The sheriff stroked his caterpillar-like facial hair and narrowed his beady eyes. "She could've taken the drug on her own. Kids these days are crazy enough to shoot themselves up with ketamine to get high."

Lifting her arms from beneath the blanket, Bexley pushed on the sweatshirt's sleeves. Red welts circled her wrists. "I suppose you're going to tell me those same *crazy kids* also shoot themselves up while handcuffed."

Swearing under his breath, Grayson pressed his mouth against her ear. "Don't say anything more." He straightened while gently squeezing her shoulder. "Unless you're officially charging her with something, you have to release her."

"The DA's inclined to hold her on the charge of civil harassment. I understand there's been a restraining order filed on behalf of Kappa Kappa Delta."

"Does that mean DA Jenkins is claiming *I* harassed *him*?" Bexley asked with a snort.

Grayson squeezed her shoulder in a way that felt like a stern warning. "Jenkins has to remove himself from the case," he told the sheriff. "His involvement in this matter is personal."

"That's up for the judge to decide." Standing, Sheriff Blair rested a hand on his protruding belly. "I suggest you get yourself a good attorney, young lady. You're gonna need one to keep yourself from serving life for murder. Best be countin' your lucky stars the State of California suspended the death penalty."

As FAR AS Bexley was concerned, the one good thing about being picked up by the Sheriff's Department was the fact that they couldn't afford to update their jailhouse, giving her a cell all to herself. The worst part was that she wasn't surrounded by the upper-class residents of Papaya Springs. After they'd confiscated her belongings and issued a standard uniform that stunk like mildew, she was subject to the cries and pleas of her fellow inmates as she unsuccessfully attempted to sleep off the lingering effects of the ketamine.

"Let me the hell outta here! My baby girl needs her momma!"

"That son-of-a-bitch deserved more than an ass-whooping!"

"Please, mister! Just one hit. Just a little something to take the edge off."

Grayson had been reluctant to release her from his embrace once a deputy came into the interrogation room to formally book her, but she assured him she'd be okay and sent him home. His last words to her were, "Try not to make any more enemies."

A tiny sliver of her soul—most likely the confused part of her still doped up with ketamine—wished he would've been stubborn and refused to leave. The wiser, non-drugged side of her was still angry that he'd scolded her the same way as her father.

Was she one of those women who subconsciously need to be controlled or punished? The idea was laughable. Maybe Grayson had just changed, and wasn't the right person for her. Or maybe she was beginning to understand they were in an unhealthy relationship, and she needed to move on.

"Squires, you have a visitor."

Bexley shot to her feet, meeting the uniformed deputy at the door as he inserted his key. On first glance, she knew the square-jawed man with ape-like features would make a terrible host during her stay simply by the wicked look embedded deep inside his cold stare.

"*Someone's* looking better," he commented wryly. "You put on a hell of an act earlier. Do you do the fake drunk girl thing at parties too? Pretend you're too drunk for consent in order to save your reputation?"

"Spoken like the kind of scumbag who would hide evidence to get a bro off rape-charges."

The man glared her down as he stepped back. "I'm looking forward to making your stay with us *real* comfortable."

So much for heeding Grayson's warning, Bexley thought, ready to kick herself.

Though it was her first time in the belly of the facility, it was easy enough to spot the visitor's section once they passed down a long hallway. Kiersten sat alone within the brick walls, perched on the kind of folding tables they had in high school lunch rooms. She smiled warmly when she spotted Bexley, and perched on the edge of the bench.

The guard's eyes swept over Kiersten with appreciation. "Don't know why you're wasting your time with this one, but you have ten minutes, sugar."

Kiersten slapped her hands over her heart. "Aw! You remind me of my pops…he'd always call me sugar too!"

"Guess that explains why the two of you are friends," the guard snarled. Bexley heard him mutter, *"bitches"* under his breath as he slammed the door behind him.

Turning back to Kiersten, Bexley eyed the bag at her friend's side. "Hope you've got something in there to accessorize with this jumpsuit. This orange isn't working with my pallid complexion."

Lips pinched together, Kiersten stood and they met in the middle for an embrace. "I know you didn't hurt anyone," she whispered.

"That makes three of us who believe in my innocence."

Backing away, Kiersten shook her head. "Don't forget Cineste and J.J. They're worried sick. Your sister called me as soon as Grayson told them the news. She said she knew without question you'd been set up, and wanted to know how she could help."

Admittedly, Bexley felt a rush of relief when hearing her sister and J.J. were also on Team Free Bexley. "Assuming I make it out of here, you'll have to let her know I may be taking her up on that offer."

Kiersten picked a hair off Bexley's uniform. "Any idea who might've done this to you?"

"If I wrote out a list of suspects, it'd be longer than a CVS receipt. But I have a pretty good idea who's to blame."

There was a brief knock on the door before they were joined by a tall, angular man in a sharp gray suit. His jet black hair was styled in the current trend, and he omitted a wonderfully rich, spicy scent. His gaze and posture indicated he was worldly, but the slight roundness to his cheeks made him appear closer to his late twenties/early thirties. Dark eyes flickered from Kiersten to Bexley as he passed a brown leather briefcase from one hand to the other. "I'm Luke Jacobs. Grayson hired me to get you the hell out of here."

Kiersten's jaw lagged. "Are you wearing a Brioni?" It didn't take a genius to catch the way the attorney's impeccable style had impressed her. And it was impossible not to notice how the handsome attorney was studying Kiersten with interest.

"I'm sorry, but who are you?" Luke asked, his gruff timbre becoming lighter with every word.

"My fiercely loyal friend," Bexley replied.

Kiersten offered him her hand, smiling shyly when he shook it. "Kiersten Douglas. Please do right by my girl. She shouldn't be here."

Luke held her gaze. "Don't worry, Miss Douglas. I'll get them to drop the charges."

Bexley hoped he meant it, and it wasn't just something he was saying to impress her friend.

CHAPTER FIFTEEN

Monday morning, Bexley was as nervous as she'd ever remembered being when Deputy Danks led her into the small courtroom through a side door. She all at once froze, unable to move. What if she wasn't brave enough to survive facing what was coming? What if she was sent to prison? The stale air and stillness of the room took her breath away, and unsettled her stomach.

"Deep breaths, Bexley," Danks whispered, setting a hand on her back. "It'll be okay."

The deputy had been especially attentive to her needs whenever he was on duty, and she would be eternally grateful for his kindness. The other deputies treated her…well, like a dangerous criminal.

She nodded and stepped inside the courtroom, lips sucked into her mouth. Tears stung her eyes when she saw Grayson, Kiersten, Cineste, and Alex sitting in the front row of the gallery directly behind where Luke Jacobs stood. Each of them greeted her with terse smiles or nods. Kiersten gave her a thumbs up right before Bexley sat in the chair her attorney had pulled out.

Kiersten had given her a simple gray pantsuit and a navy dress shirt to go underneath. By the stitching and luxurious feel of the material, she suspected it was more expensive than anything she owned. The professional look was completed when Bexley slicked her hair back into a neat bun. She had laughed to herself when she caught her reflection in a hallway window, deciding if she ever needed to pose as an attorney, she'd know just the look.

"Good morning," Luke told her in a low voice, settling in beside her. "You're looking much better today." He briefly touched her arm. "Like I said yesterday, today's hearing will be pretty informal, so just relax. Your only role in this is to tell the judge you're pleading not guilty. After I get you out on bail, we'll focus on a game plan."

Behind them, a door squeaked open. Bexley turned to see J.J. slip inside the courtroom, wearing his Sunday best. The moment their eyes met, his kind eyes softened and one side of his mouth quirked with a little grin. Seeing his reaction and knowing he was there for her somehow made the tightness in her chest dissipate.

"All rise," a male bailiff announced in a deep, booming voice.

Bexley stood along with Luke as a petite, white-haired woman in a black robe entered through a door behind the bench.

"The Currie County Court is now in session," the bailiff recited, as if having said it a thousand times before. "The Honorable Cassandra Brooks residing."

The judge regarded the audience over a pair of tortoise shell reading glasses. "You may be seated." The courtroom filled with the sound of everyone else settling in around them as Bexley and her attorney remained standing. The judge surveyed the documents in her hands, deep wrinkles surrounding her features stretching wider. "The first case this morning is State versus Bexley Squires, case number CR-one nine-five three oh nine," she continued in a steady, authoritative tone. "Miss Squires, you are charged with the following: attempted murder in the first degree, and assault with a deadly weapon. How do you plead?"

"Not guilty, Your Honor." Bexley was surprised by the steadiness of her own voice after hearing the horrifying charges spoken aloud. Especially when she'd been awake all night, wondering how easily she could be convicted of murder, whether or not she had done anything.

Judge Brooks adjusted her glasses. "Who is representing the state and the defendant?"

The tall, slim woman in a black suit standing behind the table across from Bexley tucked her curly auburn hair behind an ear, and turned to throw Bexley a dark, pointed look as she said, "Assistant District Attorney Mariah Holmes representing the State, Your Honor."

Shots fired, Bexley thought to herself. Although ADA Holmes gave off a shady vibe that would suggest she was the type to lure little boys and girls into a home made of gingerbread, She assumed the gesture had been personally passed along to her by the DA.

"Luke Jacobs for the defendant, Your Honor," Luke volleyed.

The judge scribbled something onto the paper in front of her. "The next hearing will be arranged by the county clerk's office, and notice will be sent to all parties. Is there anything else we need to cover at this hearing?"

"I'd like to request bail, Your Honor," Luke said.

"*Your Honor,*" Attorney Holmes replied with a sarcastic laugh, "the State *strenuously* objects to bail. I'm here today because the DA had to recuse himself based on a harassment restraining order involving the defendant! Letting a suspected violent criminal roam the streets of Papaya Springs would be ill-advised! This community cannot afford to have another Dean Halliwell on the loose!"

Bexley squeezed her eyes shut before she made the mistake of rolling them in plain view of the judge.

"Don't let her get under your skin," Luke whispered into her ear. "She's purposely trying to get a reaction."

"Would a certain hand gesture qualify as a reaction?" Bexley whispered back.

"*Your Honor,*" Luke retorted, "at this point the State is unable to produce a victim, or provide any evidence *whatsoever* linking my client to this alleged missing young woman. My client was drugged and left alongside the highway. Miss Squires resides with a respected police detective who has maintained a spotless history in the five years since his promotion. And I'd like to add that since my client's return to Papaya Springs, she has helped the great state of California successfully prosecute a handful of criminals, *including* Dean Halliwell. Suggesting she's a threat to this community is nothing short of preposterous."

The judge's eyes shifted to Bexley. "I'm inclined to set bail at one hundred thousand. Defendant is ordered to stay away from anyone associated with the alleged victim, and remain within the limits of this county. If she fails to report for the next hearing, a warrant will be issued for her arrest. We're adjourned."

The door to the courtroom creaked again. Bexley glanced back to see J.J. was gone. She suspected he wasn't interested in a sappy reunion, and was merely there to show his support.

"Thank *God*," Kiersten said behind her, releasing a loud sigh.

Bexley turned to throw her little tribe a shaky smile as Danks rushed forward to remove her handcuffs. She wasn't sure what to say when her sister flung her arms around her. Most of all, she was embarrassed that they were put in that situation. She could've kissed Luke for getting her out on bail, but she suspected Kiersten would be doing it on her behalf soon enough the way she made eyes at the handsome attorney. "You're a lifesaver, Luke."

"Let us know when you're up for company," Cineste said to Bexley. "We can bring you something to eat and a bottle of wine—whatever you need."

It was on the tip of Bexley's tongue to ask if she was no longer welcome at their condo when Grayson embraced her next. Although she wasn't entirely sure she wanted to stay at his place, she melted against his hard chest. Even if he was an overly controlling alpha male who wanted to control her life and treated her like a kid, she had missed him. "I'll be waiting for you in the parking lot right outside the jail. The nightmare will be over soon, Bex." He kissed the top of her head before stepping back.

"Come to my office first thing in the morning," Luke told them while shaking Grayson's hand, then Bexley's. "We'll go over what happens next."

As she was being led from the courtroom by Danks, Bexley caught Kiersten and Luke lingering alone, talking over the bar that separates the counselors' tables from the audience. Kiersten giggled behind a hand held to her lips. Bexley hoped they found more in common than taste in fashion and good looks, because they'd make a good pair.

Once she was discharged, she assumed she wouldn't have to collect anything as Luke had mentioned everything she had in her possession when brought in had been processed as evidence. So after she signed her terms of release papers, she was surprised when the female deputy behind the glass handed her a paper Verizon bag with a brand new smart phone inside. Bexley was about to tell the woman it didn't belong to her when she noticed a handwritten note scrawled on the side of the bag.

Figured you'd need a new one. They tell me everything from your account has been transferred over some "cloud" so you should be good to go. I'll be in touch soon. We have serious work ahead of us. - J.J.

Bexley's cheeks warmed with emotion. The old man's endless generosity and belief in her nearly made up for all the years she'd been neglected by her father.

"The man who left that also posted your bail bond," the woman told her. "Just sign here, and you're good to go."

"Thank you," Bexley choked out while taking a pen the woman offered.

Before meeting Grayson in the parking lot, she wiped the tears from her eyes. Her tribe was small, but they were loyal and fierce as hell.

IN THE PARKING lot behind the sheriff's office, Bexley relaxed in the passenger's seat of Grayson's open-top Bronco. She couldn't wait to step into his dual-nozzle shower. It would take the hottest water tolerable to scorch the memories of being confined in the cell for two solid days with nothing more than her paranoia and the desperate pleas of the other inmates to keep her company.

Grayson rested a hand behind Bexley's head, regarding her with an adoring look. "J.J. and I are going to help you piece together what happened that night, Bex. We'll start by tracking down this alleged victim ourselves."

Bexley's eyes flickered downward. She was unable to take the intensity behind that look. "But the judge said—"

"I know what she said. I'm not leaving your fate up to that bumbling idiot Sheriff. He's had it out for you since Halliwell was arrested. But my involvement will have to remain low-key. Not just because the lieutenant would fire me if I were caught, but because I could be charged as being an accessory. And I can't protect you if I'm behind bars."

"It's not your job to protect *me*," she reminded him in a gentle tone. "You're paid to protect *the public*. If you'd get that fact sorted out in your head, most of the problems between us might go away."

"Do you really believe that?" he asked quietly.

"That I don't need your protection, or the fact that you constantly coddle me is a major obstacle in our relationship?" Her fists clenched in her lap. "I chose a dangerous profession, Grayson. Same as you. I appreciate it when you have my back, but telling me what I can and can't do isn't going to fly. *Ever*."

Grayson brought both hands to the steering wheel, gripping it tightly. Irritation ticked through his jaw. "I think this is a conversation for later… when things aren't so complicated. Right now we need to focus on clearing your name, and figuring out who set you up. It goes without saying that neither of us can have any contact with the girls in the sorority, so we'll have to use other resources. Your sister has already volunteered to go undercover."

Letting out a deep breath, Bexley nodded thoughtfully. Although she hated putting her sister into another dangerous situation, she was aware their resources were limited. "Once we know more about this missing girl, Cineste can reach out to her friends. Luke told me her name is Dayna Stryker, but I don't remember ever coming across anyone by that name. Does it ring any bells with you?"

"J.J. already looked into it. She's one of two daughters of Phillip Stryker, a CEO you brought down with the Boys' Club. He served four months for solicitation." As he started the engine, Grayson glanced at her over his shoulder, one eyebrow raised. "Wanna take a wild guess where you can find his other daughter?"

She quirked an eyebrow. "Guessing I can rule out Disney World."

"She's the President of Kappa Kappa Delta."

Of course she would be the sorority president. A small

flame of anger ignited in Bexley's belly. "Would this other daughter's name happen to be Alicia?"

"You've met her?"

"Yeah, and she mentioned Daddy Dearest once we were properly introduced. Those girls were hell-bent on making me pay, Grayson. The Mayor and DA too. I'd bet my life that they're behind this. We just need a fail-proof way to prove it."

"We will," he promised.

"What do you know about Judge Brooks and that assistant DA? Do you think they can be trusted, or could they be easily bought? I got a Harvey Dent kind of vibe from that Mariah Holmes woman."

While maneuvering into the street, Grayson grunted. "I noticed the way she was looking at you in court. I'd say she's suspect to playing dirty. Judge Brooks is a different story. She has a history of being hard-nosed, but more importantly, fair." He reached out to squeeze Bexley's hand. "We're going to find this girl. That should be all the proof we need to make the state drop the charges against you."

CINESTE TRADED her shift with another hostess at the restaurant, and was standing in Grayson's kitchen by the time Bexley took a long shower and changed. She brought Alex along, which annoyed Bexley to no end, but she supposed they were becoming a packaged deal.

"You look exhausted," Cineste commented, eyeing Bexley's face. "Sure you want to do this now, and not wait until after you've had some decent rest?"

"I won't sleep until we find that girl," Bexley insisted.

Grayson's phone rang. He answered it with a low greeting before heading into the other room.

Bexley held her sister's worried expression. "Cin, there's something I've been meaning to tell you. Dad came by my office last week…with Hillary. She told him she'd been assaulted, but after a little digging around, I discovered that she was trying to cover up an affair. I guess I just thought you should know."

Shock registered in Cineste's features, then she let out a hollow laugh. "Serves that son-of-a-bitch right for picking a woman closer to *your* age. How did he react when you told him?"

"Same as always…cold…detached." Bexley

shrugged. "He said he'd send a check for my services. Doubt I'll hear from him again."

"Wish you would've let me deliver the news," Cineste grumbled, frowning. "I'd love to see him break."

Alex slung an arm around her neck, pulling her close. "Doubt that kind of thing would faze someone like him, babe." He brushed his lips over her temple. "I left my phone out in the car. Would you mind running out to grab it while I use the restroom?"

"No problem," she answered, spinning around to kiss him on the lips. Alex swatted her behind as she walked away, and she giggled like a teenager.

The second they were alone, Bexley barred her teeth. "Don't start with me, Alex. Now is definitely not the time for this."

"You don't think that shooting could've been somehow related to what happened?" Alex frowned, running his fingers through his wavy brown hair. "There was a bullet in your SUV. Grayson could run it through—"

"No!" Bexley snapped. "Let it go!"

Grayson re-entered the room, eyeing each of them with a suspicious glare. "Everything alright?"

Folding her hands tightly against her chest,

Bexley answered with a bright smile. "Not sure why *I'm* playing the role of relationship expert, but he's having a pointless spat with Cineste."

The way he watched her a beat longer before speaking again, Bexley suspected Grayson didn't believe the lie. "That was my lieutenant." His Adam's apple bobbed with a deep swallow. "Violet's awake."

CHAPTER SIXTEEN

The recently constructed hospital in the heart of Papaya Springs still carried the faint odor of fresh paint as Grayson steered them down the bright hallways covered in intricate murals of the city. Bexley was glad the old hospital had been demolished a few months back. It harbored too many bad memories of sitting with her mom during chemo sessions, waiting on pins and needles as she endured elective surgeries, and worst of all, watching her mom wither away on her death bed. But she'd already created unfavorable memories while inside the new building after being drugged.

They followed the head nurse's directions to Violet's room, stopping just outside the open door. Grayson's lieutenant paced in the hallway, grumbling into his phone. Bexley hadn't seen him in several months, and she was surprised to discover the already hefty man had put on a considerable amount of extra weight. The way his skin bunched against his suit and tie reminded her of a croissant package ready to pop. His graying hair was longer than she'd ever seen it, and he was sporting a short, salt-and-pepper beard.

When he realized he had company, his eyes remained on Bexley for a beat longer than she was prepared. It was as if he was trying to figure her out. Did he think she was guilty? She certainly *felt* guilty—for all she had put him and his family through. Finally, he looked away and motioned for them to go inside the room.

Among a sea of freshly cut flowers and mylar balloons, Violet sat upright in a hospital gown, blond hair in a sloppy knot above her head, sipping from a glass of water. Makeup-free face covered in scratches, complexion noticeably pale, she appeared several years younger, as if still in high school. Considering she had been close to death, she still looked exceptional—probably even better than Bexley.

A middle aged woman in a sensible pants suit chatted animatedly from a chair at Violet's side.

"Your Aunt Sarah and Uncle Joe are flying in from Virginia tonight. They're leaving the kids home… *thank God*. Nana and Pappy send their love, but I don't know that they'll be making the trip down. You know how much Pappy hates Papaya Springs traffic this time of year."

Grayson lightly tapped on the door. "Sorry to interrupt, Tammy. Want us to come back later?"

"Grayson! Of course not!" The woman stood, waving her hands through the air. Tall and slender with beautiful green eyes and dark wavy hair, she wasn't the kind of woman Bexley would've expected to be the grumpy lieutenant's wife. "Come on in!"

Violet's eyes slightly widened when she spotted Bexley trailing in behind Grayson with a bouquet of roses and daisies in hand.

"You must be Grayson's girlfriend," Tammy said to Bexley, offering a warm smile. "It's so nice to finally meet you. I've been begging my husband and Grayson to set up a dinner meeting so I could finally meet the woman who tamed this handsome one's heart." She patted Grayson's cheek and laughed merrily. "It's so sweet of you to spend so much time with our girl. I should've known you'd be one of her first visitors. I was just heading out to grab a cup of coffee. Can I get either of you something to drink?"

"No thank you," Bexley answered.

"Don't worry about us," Grayson told her.

Tammy patted his cheek once again. "John's making a call in the hallway, but I'm guessing you knew that already. Make yourselves at home. I won't be long."

The minute she left the room, Violet crossed her arms and glared at Grayson. *"She's* your girlfriend?" she asked, her tone accusatory. "Why didn't you tell me?"

Taking cautious steps, Bexley approached the girl. "You remember me?"

"Of course!" Violet snapped, shrinking back a little.

She has every right to be mad, Bexley reminded herself, taking a calming breath. She set the flowers on the table that stretched across the bed. "Violet, I'm so sorry this happened to you. Do you remember anything about that night after I left?"

"Every little detail you're able to recall will be helpful," Grayson added, moving in on the other side of the bed.

Violet's eyes skidded across the room. "If they found out I told you—"

"They're going down either way," Grayson assured her. "We already know you were at the Kappa Kappa Delta party that night, and someone needs to be accountable for what happened. You almost *died*, Violet. They can't get away with this without there being consequences."

The girl's tense shoulders slumped forward. "The sisters…they were super angry at me. They figured I'd told you everything even though I swore up and down that I didn't. They made me chug a bottle of vodka in the basement. I don't remember much after that." A set of tears slipped down her cheeks. She swiped them with a finger, scowling. "The dumb thing is, I'd pretty much decided before that night I was going to leave them. I mean…it wasn't the first time they made me do something extreme. Not by a long-shot. I only stayed because of Kayla."

"It's my fault," Bexley told her. "I should've called the police before they told me to leave. They would've brought them in on charges of theft. I shouldn't have left you alone."

"They still would've found a way to get back at me," Violet said, lifting one shoulder.

Grayson glanced back and forth between them.

"The only one responsible is whoever made you drink that vodka. Who was it, Violet?"

"I don't know…there were so many of them. They surrounded me, chanting *'drink it up! drink it up!'* until I finally gave in. I just wanted them to stop."

"You can take your time coming up with a list of names," Grayson said, patting her arm, "but I'm going to need them eventually. In the meantime, what else did they make you do? What kind of things went on during hazing?"

Violet rubbed her bare forearms. "Do we have to talk about that?"

"Hazing is illegal for a reason," he reminded her gently. "We don't have to talk about it right now, but I have some other questions that might help Bexley out of a jam. Is that alright?"

She glanced over at Bexley, as if asking for her opinion. The gesture felt like an alliance, as if she had already forgiven Bexley.

Bexley replied with a little smile. "It's okay if you're not feeling up to it—"

"No, it's okay," Violet decided.

"Do you know Dayna Stryker?" Grayson asked.

Violet squinted and titled her head. "You mean Alicia's little sister?"

"Yeah. What can you tell us about her?"

"Not much." Violet paused to take a drink of her water. "I only saw her once. She dropped by the house last week and got into this ugly fight with Alicia. I got the impression right away that she's a real brat though." She set the water down and rubbed her forearms. "Dayna went off on Alicia because she'd told their dad that Dayna dropped out of school. It sounded like Dayna has a habit of doing stuff to upset their dad."

"Did they mention Bexley at all during their fight?" Grayson asked.

"No. The fight was pretty short-lived. After Dayna said she told their dad that Alicia has chlamydia, Alicia caught us listening in, and got crazy upset." Sniffling, she looked down. "They threw us into the trunk of a car and took us to this creek…made us get down in the mud to do push-ups and stuff."

While Grayson said something to Violet, faint memories tried to break through Bexley's thoughts.

She'd been in a trunk.

She'd heard running water.

There was a musty basement.

Before she could properly process the memories, she found herself clutching Violet's arm. "Was there a house near the creek? Like something old, maybe one that was abandoned?"

"Yeah. A real creepy looking one." Violet pulled away from Bexley to wrap her arms around herself. "How'd you know?"

"That's where they took me the night I was kidnapped," Bexley told Grayson. "I remember now…they took me down into a basement…they were all wearing disturbing masks."

Grayson nodded his chin and reached for his cell phone. "I'll have my office run a property search for the Stryker family. Maybe they own something that fits that description." Bexley caught a glint of excitement in his expression as he exited the room, phone held to his ear.

Violet sucked in a sharp gasp at Bexley's side. "Wait. You were *kidnapped?* When?"

"It's a long story."

"You think the Stryker family had something to do with it?"

Bexley sighed thoughtfully, exhausted from dealing with rich assholes. "I'm being accused of hurting Dayna, and she's allegedly missing. Problem is, I was drugged, and don't remember much of anything."

"Alicia's sadistic and bat-shit crazy. I wouldn't be surprised if the rest of that family is the same way."

"The night I met you, there was a fresh abrasion on your face," Bexley gently reminded her. She set her hand on Violet's shoulder. "Did Alicia do that to you? Was she the one who made you drink the vodka?"

A fat tear spilled down Violet's cheek. She slowly nodded with great trepidation. "She took pictures of me wearing that dog collar...said she'd tell the cops I took it if I told anyone, or tried to leave. It's the same threat she was holding over Kayla's head." Mouth pressed in a tight line, she flicked her tears with the side of her hand. "I should've come forward anyway. My dad's a cop... he would've made things right. But I knew my parents would be upset that I had joined a sorority. You wanna know the most ironic part about all this? My mom's best friend in college died during a hazing ritual. They got her black-out drunk, and she fell down a flight of stairs. That's why they're so dead set against greek life. And that's why I refused to leave Kayla behind. I keep waiting for an 'I told you so' from my mom, but she's been cool about it."

"The 'I told you so' might still be coming, but

your mom quite obviously cares about you," Bexley said with a soft smile. "She's probably just relieved you're alive. You gave everyone quite a scare."

"Will you check on Kayla for me? Make sure she's okay?" More tears swarmed Violet's sky blue eyes. "I've left a few messages, but she hasn't answered."

"I have to stay away from the sorority, but I'll ask someone to stop by to see her. I have a feeling it won't be long before all hell breaks loose for Alicia and the other Deltas. Campus will most likely shut the house down until the investigation is complete."

Violet sniffled again. "Oh my god, they'll come after me again."

"No, they won't," Bexley promised in a grave tone. She lightly squeezed the girl's shoulder. "Violet, I'm going to do everything I can to ensure Alicia Stryker and her band of idiots don't terrorize another pledge ever again. Just promise me you won't let them intimidate you when it comes time to testify against them. You were strong enough to survive this—you'll survive whatever comes next too."

"Yeah, okay." Then a forced laugh fell from Violet's lips. "You know, you're pretty cool. I hope like hell they find Dayna and make that spoiled little brat pay for doing this to you."

Bexley laughed along with her. "That makes two of us."

Grayson came trotting back into the room with a hard expression as he held Bexley's gaze. "Luke just called, told us to swing by his office right away. He said it's urgent."

Bexley touched Violet's arm. "Take care of yourself, Violet. I'll be in touch."

In the hallway, Lieutenant Baker ended his call behind them with a grunted, "Goodbye." Then they heard his leather dress shoes pound the linoleum as he took off after them. "I've requested a special prosecutor be assigned to go after the sorority. They're waiting for a judge to be appointed so they can file the necessary paperwork."

Bexley spun around to face him. "Violet told me Alicia Stryker made her drink the vodka," she said. "She's scared of what might happen to her, but I think I convinced her to testify against Alicia."

"You'd be wise to stay as far away from this as possible," the lieutenant advised. "The Stryker family seems intent on stopping you."

Grayson crossed his arms and side-eyed his

boss. "Both Violet and Bexley saw an old house by a creek after they were taken out of a trunk. Do you happen to know offhand if Phillip Stryker owns any abandoned property?"

For a moment, the lieutenant scratched at his beard. Then something sparked in his gaze. "Matter of fact, there was something mentioned during his trial about some land he had inherited. It only came up because DA Jenkins asked to be recused from Stryker's case…said they hunted together regularly on Stryker's property."

"Call the special prosecutor," Grayson told him. "Have them request a search warrant for the property. Have them look for Halloween masks, and anything containing traces of ketamine—a vile or a used needle." He snagged Bexley's hand, and started turning his back on the lieutenant. "Tell them to call me when they get there."

"Where are you going?" the lieutenant called after them. "I could use your help on this!"

Bexley felt a tug of appreciation, knowing Grayson was putting her situation before his job.

THE JACOBS & Johnson Law Firm was only a few blocks from the hospital in a small brick building nestled between the impressive skyscrapers downtown like a squatter that refused to leave. The interior was clean and modern chic: white walls, minimal furniture, small pops of color, and framed candids from around the city. A friendly receptionist around Bexley's age stood behind a white desk to greet them with a smile. "You must be—"

Luke materialized from around the corner. "I've got it, Ginny." Expression grim, he pointed in Bexley's direction. "Come this way."

Her heart thundered as she trailed behind Luke and Grayson. *Please don't let Dayna be dead, please don't let Dayna be dead, please don't let Dayna be dead* she chanted in her head.

Once they were seated in his office that mirrored the feel of the lobby, Luke steepled his fingers to his forehead. "We have a serious problem. The lab results came in. The blood in the car matched the blood on the knife they found Bexley holding."

Bexley tried to swallow, but her throat wouldn't work.

"That doesn't prove anything," Grayson grumbled. "It's still circumstantial evidence."

"There's more." Luke's jaw flexed as he looked at Bexley. "Have any of your memories from that night resurfaced?"

"Just now…we were visiting the Delta pledge that was admitted for alcohol poisoning, and she claimed the Deltas put her in a trunk and took her to a creek. I remembered something about a trunk and a creek by an old house the night I was kidnapped."

"My people are looking into it," Grayson added.

Bexley eyed Luke, wiping her sweaty palms on her shorts. "Why are you asking? What else do you know?"

"They found Bexley's fingerprints on the steering wheel. The prosecutor believes it proves she was inside that vehicle. *Driving*."

Bexley's stomach dropped. What if she was wrong about what had happened? What if she *had* hurt Dayna after all?

"Before or after they pumped her full of hallucinogens?" Grayson roared, rising to his feet. "She didn't do anything to that girl! You don't know Bex like I do, Luke! She isn't capable of doing this kind of thing! And there's still no goddamned motive! She's never even met Dayna!"

"Hey! I believe you!" Luke yelled back. "But *someone* is hell-bent on sending her away!" He leaned forward, holding Grayon's angry glare and lowering his voice. "Unless you want to see Bexley go down for this bogus crime, you need to find this girl. As soon as humanly possible."

CHAPTER SEVENTEEN

B exley would've risked her life for everyone gathered around her in the conference room of Stronghold Investigations. The space was mostly used for the three employees to grab a quick bite in peace, and included a refrigerator and microwave. J.J. had snagged a reasonable oak table at an estate sale that seated eight, and served that day's purpose well. Bexley's stomach hadn't stopped twisting since they left Luke's office, and seeing her friends gathered only increased her anxieties when it dawned on her that the same crew would likely be the only ones in attendance at her funeral one day.

"I've asked you all here as this investigation has taken an urgent turn," J.J. said, walking around the room to hand everyone the same sheet of paper. "This here is a list of all the contacts on Dayna Stryker's cell phone. I'm gonna need each and every one of you to study this list, see if you can find a pattern or anything that stands out. If any of you have a connection to anyone on this list, I'm asking you to use it to help us in any way possible. We need to use every resource available to locate this girl. *ASAP*."

Bexley watched Cineste pull her bottom lip into her mouth as her eyes scanned over the lengthy list. She hated that she was bringing her sister into another dire situation. What if the same people who hurt Bexley went after Cineste next?

At Cineste's side, Alex scowled. "Is there anyone in SoCal she *didn't* know?"

"It could take us *days* to contact all these people," Deputy Danks agreed, letting the papers in his hand slip onto the table in front of him. "We don't have that kind of time. The prosecutor is out for Bexley's blood. They're probably amending the charges as we speak."

"Oh my god, *people*," Kiersten sang, waving her sheet through the air. "The answer to this is so obvious. If this girl ran off into hiding, her friends will be fiercely loyal, and you aren't going to be able to bribe a bunch of rich girls with money. We need to find someone on this list who doesn't feel a loyalty toward her."

"You mean like her dentist?" Alex asked.

Cineste lightly elbowed his ribs. "No, silly. Someone she can actually speak to in confidence."

"Yet someone *other* than a psychologist," Kiersten agreed. "They'd be bound by confidentiality laws."

"Yeah," Cineste continued, sitting a little taller. Her lips curved upward. "The kind of person that compels almost every girl in America to spill their life story."

Bexley wasn't following their line of thought. "Guys, the suspense is killing me. Who are we talking about here?"

"Hair stylist!" Cineste and Kiersten answered in unison, throwing each other the same goofy grin.

"They may have a valid point," Grayson agreed. "We just have to decide what angle to use. Do we send one of the girls in there, posing as a nosy customer, or straight-up ask this stylist what she knows about Dayna?"

The door to the conference room suddenly

opened. Captain Ferguson appeared in the doorway. "What did I miss?"

Bexley audibly gulped with the sight of her father in casual attire—the kind of polo shirt and khakis he'd wear to the golf course. There was a softness to his green eyes that she didn't think she'd seen since she was a little girl.

"What are you doing here?" Bexley managed.

All eyes were on the captain as he stepped into the room with his arms held behind his back in typical military fashion. "Your employer called, said you were in some trouble, and needed my help."

Jaw held tight, Bexley threw J.J. an accusatory glare that screamed *how dare you*, but the old man simply shrugged, as if to say *can't help it, you need 'im*.

"Better late than never," Cineste huffed. She rose from the table and marched across the room, shoving her sheet of paper into her father's hands. "This is a list of contacts for a girl they've accused Bexley of killing. Her name is Dayna Stryker. We know it's all bullshit, so we're going to find this girl to prove nothing happened."

"Accused of *killing?*" their father repeated, glancing around the room until his gaze fell back on Bexley. "What the hell is going on?"

"It's a long story," Bexley said. "To summarize,

I've managed to cross even *more* powerful people in Papaya Springs, and they want to see me stopped. If you have any doubt whether or not I did this, you can—"

Her father held up the palm of his hand. "If you say you're innocent, then I believe you."

Bexley's wide eyes met Cineste's. They both batted their lashes, stunned beyond words. What happened to the cynical dictator they'd known since birth?

"Great," Cineste finally said, her tone flat.

"Great," Bexley echoed with the same amount of enthusiasm.

Their father's gaze skipped from Cineste to Bexley. "May I have a moment with you two in the hallway?"

Bexley looked to J.J. as if awaiting his approval, and the old man dipped his chin. "Go ahead, darlin'. We'll brainstorm ideas on how to approach this stylist until you get back."

The room fell silent as Cineste and Bexley followed their father out to the hallway. Before he turned back to face them, Cineste gave Bexley's wrist an urgent squeeze. Bexley understood her sister's trepidation—she was just as unsure of the situation.

"Hillary's no longer living with me," he began, eyes trained on his perfectly shined loafers. "Something about this nonsense with her made me realize how skewed my priorities have become since your mother's death. The Navy has always come first, and it's time for a change...before it's too late." Then his eyes traveled upward to meet Bexley's. "I'm retiring at the end of next month. I'd be honored if you both could attend the ceremony. The base has planned a casual reception downtown for later that night, but I'd like to take you out for dinner beforehand, if you're up for it."

The overload of information sent Bexley reeling. What was it about his trophy wife that stirred human emotions from the man? Why hadn't the realization come when his youngest went missing, or his oldest nearly died?

Shaking the dazed thoughts from her head, she looped her arm through Cineste's. "Um...yeah," she told him. "Of course. We'll be there."

It was a risky promise to make. If they didn't find Dayna Stryker soon, she'd be kissing that kind of freedom goodbye.

IT WAS DECIDED that Kiersten and Bexley would interrogate Dayna's stylist while the others tackled the contact list. Kiersten would have the proper charm needed to schmooze Papaya Springs's finest, and Bexley would know the right questions to ask.

Inside the salon, several of the city's finest women waited on black leather couches, flipping through celebrity magazines and sipping from champagne flutes. Their curious eyes sized Kiersten and Bexley up as they entered, some not bothering to hide their disapproval. State-of-the-art hair dryers and rows of white leather client chairs among white walls, oversized mirrors, and ornate chandeliers gave the space the feel of a high-end boutique. Bexley guessed the cost of their services would be astronomical before they approached the glass receptionist's desk, and she noticed a price list.

"Three hundred for a haircut?" she mused under her breath. "Does that rate include a night's stay at the Royal?"

A tall woman with creamy dark skin and beautiful black curls approached them behind the desk. She perfectly matched the salon's decor in a slim-fitting white dress with a thin black ribbon around her waist. She first threw Kiersten a friendly smile.

Then her lips pursed when she noticed Bexley. "Can I *help* you?"

"I'm the one who called about an emergency appointment with Merry," Kiersten explained.

The woman's expression eased somewhat as she crossed her arms and regarded Kiersten. "Ah, yes. Miss Douglas. You're lucky we were able to fit you in. Merry has a waiting list out to the end of the year."

"It helps having connections in the right places," Kiersten responded, winking.

The woman's skeptical gaze skipped back onto Bexley. "I'm assuming the appointment is for your friend?"

Bexley pointed to her head. "Apparently twenty dollars does *not* get the job done right."

The receptionist huffed under her breath. "Follow me."

Bexley was taken to a room in the back where an assistant stylist shampooed her hair and placed a warm towel over her face while Kiersten watched on. Bexley tried to pull information from the young girl, but she wasn't too keen on chatting. Nearly half an hour later, the assistant took her to an elaborate booth. She settled into the plush stool as the woman secured a cape around her neck, and gave the women each a glass of champagne.

"Here's hoping this is worth it," Bexley told Kiersten, clinking their glasses together. "I'm a little ashamed to admit I could get used to this lifestyle."

Moments later, they were joined by the vibrant woman they'd seen pictured on the salon's website. Merry Echols wasn't anything like one would expect to find in a town of privileged upperclass. Dark hair shaved on one side, numerous visible tattoos, edgy makeup. In 4-inch heels and a polka dotted Betty dress, hair expertly styled with a white knotted headband, petite features among oversized eyes, she was strikingly beautiful. Bexley suspected even the crème de la crème of Papaya Springs were unable to deny the woman's irresistible aura when she smiled.

"Hey, I'm Merry," she told Bexley, offering an inked hand. "I hear you have an emergency. What can I do for you today?"

As Bexley shook her hand, she decided to deviate from the plan and go the straightforward route. She sensed Merry wasn't the type to tolerate anything less. "Actually, Merry, I'm here to see what you can tell me about Dayna Stryker."

"And to get her hair fixed," Kiersten blurted,

stepping in beside the stool. "Maybe something shorter…with layers."

Bexley shot Kiersten a questionable look. She hadn't agreed to anything quite so drastic.

"You have great bone structure. I think I know just the look." Merry ran her fingers through Bexley's wet hair, meeting her gaze in the mirror. "I heard about Dayna's disappearance in the news." She spread a hand over her heart. "It's so tragic. First thing I thought to myself was 'oh my god, I hope Dean Halliwell didn't break out of jail'. Can you imagine?"

Bexley gnawed on her tongue, fighting the temptation to point out the important fact that Dean's victims were all brunettes. "How long have you been doing Dayna's hair?"

"I'd say a good two years." Merry continued chatting as she retrieved a comb and scissors from a set of drawers. "Her hair's silky as a baby's bottom, but it's thick enough that it doesn't matter. She's one lucky *chica*."

"When did you last see her?" Bexley asked.

Merry's lips twisted as she ran the comb through the ends of Bexley's hair. "She came in for a balayage a couple of weeks ago."

"Did she tell you she was dropping out of college?"

"She mentioned she was toying with the idea of leaving Papaya Springs," Merry answered, shrugging. "She wanted to get as far away from her family as possible. I don't think she got along with any of them, and her dad sounds pretty controlling."

"Did she ever say anything about a boyfriend? Maybe someone she was hiding from her dad?"

"She told me she was seeing someone, but never went into any real details aside from saying he was crazy hot," Merry said as she began snipping Bexley's hair. "But the last time she was here, there was a beautiful S.O.B. waiting outside by the curb with a motorcycle helmet in hand. She was right about him…the guy was dreamy as hell. We're talkin' wet-your-britches gorgeous. Wavy brown hair, the kind of sexy eyes a girl can get lost in. I wouldn't be surprised if the guy was trying to make it in Hollywood."

"Anything else you can remember about him?"

"He had on one of those leather vests that they wear in motorcycle clubs."

Bexley's interest was officially piqued. It was the classic story…girl with daddy issues runs away with a bad boy. *Just as Cineste had once planned to do with Alex.* If they could narrow this biker down to a certain club, she was willing to bet she could prove her theory. "Do you remember seeing any logos on the vest?"

Merry focused on Bexley's hair as her fingers continued to flip and clip with precision. "Yeah…on the back…there were stars and an eagle holding an American flag in its claws. Real patriotic-like. I didn't catch the words around it though."

Pulse hammering against her throat, Bexley eyed Kiersten in the mirror. For the first time since she was arrested, they had a tangible lead.

"I'll call Grayson," Kiersten offered with a nod, pulling her phone from her handbag and stepping away.

"Do you mind giving me your cell number? You know, in case I think of any other questions?" Bexley asked Merry once they were alone.

"Not at all."

"You've been a tremendous help, Merry. Thanks for agreeing to fit me in."

The stylist leaned down until her mouth was level with Bexley's ear. "Just between you and me, that little snot comes in here, bragging about her new thousand dollar handbag, then leaves a lousy ten dollar tip. I hope you find her, Bexley."

With a start, Bexley watched the woman's reflection as she resumed the transformation. At no point had either Kiersten or Bexley given her name to the salon, and she was certain she had never met this woman.

There were more people in Bexley's corner than she thought.

CHAPTER EIGHTEEN

Bexley acknowledged the haircut had drastically changed her appearance as she caught her reflection behind the receptionist's desk. But she was even more concerned with finding the bad boy Dayna may have run off with than wondering how she was going to afford the transformation charged to her credit card. The second she stepped outside the salon with Kiersten, she dialed J.J.

"There's a veteran's motorcycle club near L.A. called Inferno Glory," his deep voice rumbled through her cell phone. "Their logo matches the description that stylist gave you. They're a good group...always doin' charity work. Heard they recently helped the FBI bring down some of their most wanted. Real stand up kind of people."

"You know them personally?"

"I was once close with the old club president… we served together in the war."

"You think he'd be open to talking with us about Dayna?"

J.J. let out a thoughtful sigh. "Remmy was murdered awhile back. Not sure who's in charge now."

"What about their clubhouse? Know where I can find it?"

"Have a pretty good idea."

A pang of excitement rippled through Bexley's belly. "Can you put Grayson on the phone?"

"Hold on."

Moments later, Grayson answered, "I know what you're thinking, but the clubhouse is outside of the county limits. You can't go there, Bex."

Bexley couldn't believe with everything going on, he was still trying to dictate her actions. She took a calming breath, knowing it wasn't the time for that discussion. "I'd bet my life that Dayna's either in hiding with this biker, or they've run off together. I have to go to this clubhouse, and see what they know. I'll wear a disguise, and stay off the beaten path. You're welcome to come along, but only if you can promise you won't try to stop me from doing whatever it takes to uncover the truth."

His tone hardened. "Come back to the office and we'll discuss this in person."

She abruptly stopped in the middle of the sidewalk, causing Kiersten to stumble to avoid a collision. "No, Grayson. There's nothing to discuss. This is how it's going to be."

"Danks won't like that you're breaking the terms of your bond," he said. "You're putting him in a tough position."

"So don't tell him!" she snapped before stabbing the END button on her screen.

Kiersten squeezed Bexley's shoulder. "You alright?"

"I have a new hairdo that cost more than my rent," Bexley grumbled, puffing out a deep breath as she turned around. "How could I be anything other than fabulous?"

"Take it easy on him, Bex. He's really struggling with the idea of you going to jail."

"I get it. What I don't get is how I'm supposed to deal with someone who is constantly invested in every move I make. You do remember I was raised by a man who controlled my every move, right?

Why do you think I fled to New York after high school? Why do you think my little sister is so messed up that she was willing to drop everything to run off with a total stranger just like Dayna?"

Folding her arms, Kiersten shrugged. "It's in Grayson's nature to protect the ones he loves. You'll never convince him to change."

"Well I'm not changing either." Exhausted by the conversation, she continued in the direction of Kiersten's car. "Come on, I have to figure out how to cozy up to a gang of bikers."

ALTHOUGH J.J. CONTINUED to swear the motorcycle club was comprised of "the good guys," it was still difficult for Bexley to agree to Cineste and Kiersten entering into their lair alongside her. It was decided Grayson and Deputy Danks would park across the street from the clubhouse, and keep a close watch on any unsavory activity. Farther down the road, J.J. kept watch for any signs of trouble that could require police involvement. Alex had been even less excited by the plan than Grayson, and had insisted on coming along when Cineste refused to back out. Bexley decided his company could work to their advantage if he posed as a veteran interested in joining their club.

They'd lucked out earlier when they'd pulled up outside the large warehouse on the edge of town, and discovered the bikers were preparing for a big party. A drum set and several guitars sat on a small stage in the back next to a large smoker that produced the heavenly aroma of pork. Picnic tables were being arranged in long rows facing the stage, and kegs were being tapped. Bexley decided it would be easy enough for them to blend in with what was likely to be an unruly crowd once Kiersten had helped them acquire the proper attire from a strip mall down the road.

"We look like we're on our way to shoot an eighties music video," Cineste whined, tugging on the black bustier she'd paired with plethora leggings. "I've never felt so ridiculous."

"This is high fashion at its finest," Kiersten scolded. "Quit fidgeting."

Bexley's scalp tingled beneath a blond wig, longing to be itched. Or maybe it was simply her nerves getting the best of her. "Don't forget what we talked about," she told them. "Alex's family was friends with their old president, and we're here trying to get a feel of what the club's all about.

Keep your eyes and ears open for any signs of Dayna. Try not to ask too many questions unless you sense someone's getting comfortable in conversation. We don't want to raise any red flags. If you discover anything useful, text me. If you run into any problems, message Grayson with a nine-one-one and get the hell outta there."

"Are you sure you want to go in there?" Alex asked, eyebrows raised her way. "This could end badly in too many ways."

Bexley threw him a warning glare before she pulled forward to the compound's gate. It was guarded by several men, including a thick-necked, older man with kinky black hair who instructed them to exit the vehicle for a pat-down. Beneath his club vest, Bexley spotted the handle of a holstered gun.

They all exhaled loudly once they were cleared to enter.

By the time they parked alongside dozens of motorcycles and found their way to the gathering, the party was in full swing. Scantily clad women—some topless—danced to the band among rowdy men donning the same vest Merry had described. There was a healthy number of women in attendance in addition to the exotic dancers. Some even wore similar leather vests featuring a different logo. Bexley broke away from the group, attempting to catalog every male club member in sight while keeping an eye out for any signs of Dayna.

She wasn't alone for long before a strikingly handsome biker with chin-length, wavy brown hair and a chiseled jaw swaggered toward where she stood. There was something in his smoldering stare that immediately set her on edge, as if he was onto her act. Her spine stiffened. *Could it be the man Merry had described?* He was exactly the kind of stereotypical bad boy she pictured someone like Dayna giving up her world to be with.

The moment he opened his velvety lips to speak, she spotted a **PRESIDENT** patch sewn onto his vest. "Hey there, darlin'. What brings you to my turf?"

From behind her fresh glass of keg beer, Bexley gave him a shy smile. "My friend, Alex, wants to join your club."

His eyebrows quirked. "Yeah? Not sure I know anyone by that name."

"He said he was friends with one of your predecessors."

"Yeah? Which one?"

"I think Alex said his name was Remmy."

Interest sparked the man's expression. "And where's this 'Alex' person?"

"He's around here somewhere…probably looking for you. He wasn't totally sure how this works."

"What about you? You come to clubhouse parties like ours often?"

"This is my first. *College* parties are more my thing." Hoping to bait him for a reaction, she added, "I'm in a sorority at PSC. Maybe you've heard of us. Kappa Kappa Delta?"

The man shrugged. "Sororities aren't anywhere on my radar, darlin'." He rose on the balls of his leather boots, motioning over the crowd with a stern look. "There seems to be a couple more stragglers like you here tonight. Did you and this Alex person bring more friends?"

Sensing trouble, Bexley paused to take a drink of the stout beer. Whether or not the man knew Dayna, he seemed easy-going. Best case scenario, he'd merely ask them to leave. *Unless his kindness was merely an act.*

She reached out to touch his arm. "Oh my god, I hope we're not breaking any of your rules by coming here with Alex! We aren't, are we? We only came because he promised it'd be fun!"

"Just wantin' to know who's among us. We've made some enemies over the years, so never can be too careful." Tipping his chin, he grinned. "Enjoy yourself, darlin'. Be sure to let me know if there's anything I can do for you and your friends."

Long after he left, Bexley continued to watch him from afar. He became heavily engaged with a sultry brunette woman wearing one of the leather vests featuring a different logo. The two of them constantly touched each other as they engaged in a group conversation, like their bodies naturally gravitated that way. Based on how they interacted, stealing glances of undeniable devotion, made it seem they had been together for quite some time and weren't merely hooking up for the night.

With every minute they spent together, Bexley was convinced he couldn't be Dayna's suitor. She wasn't up to speed on biker culture, but it seemed unlikely he was putting on a show unless he was seeing Dayna on the side. Bexley snapped a stealthy picture regardless, and sent it to Merry.

Is this the biker that was waiting for Dayna?

There was a short delay in which the bubble

with dots flashed across Bexley's screen as Merry typed out a reply.

No. His hair was shaved on the sides. But wow, that one's a looker too. Are all the men in that club hot? Maybe I should come join you.

Frustrated, Bexley spent the next hour tailing the other club members from across the crowd. Around the time she was ready to chalk the night up as a failure, she spotted a man in the club's leather cut that she hadn't seen all night. From what she could tell at a distance, he could've perfectly fit Merry's description.

The man's appearance was brief. He approached the club president, and the two men stepped away from the others. It was hard to guess the overall nature of their conversation. Both men leaned down as they spoke, concealing their faces. A small handful of minutes later, the men slapped hands in a brotherhood kind of way, and the mysterious club member turned back toward the parking lot.

Bexley darted toward Kiersten and Cineste, nudging them away from a circle of men.

"Have you heard anything we can use?" she whispered, searching both their faces.

"Not unless you're interested in several unsolicited phone numbers," Kiersten replied with a shudder. "Some of these guys are downright barbaric."

Bexley slipped her the keys to the loaner she'd been driving. "I'm going to tail someone who could be the guy we're looking for. I'll catch a ride with Grayson and Danks."

"Be careful," Cineste pleaded in an urgent tone.

As Bexley entered the parking lot, her phone buzzed inside the back pocket of her new jeans skirt. She rolled her eyes as she answered, knowing she wouldn't have to bother calling Grayson. He was already watching her every step through a pair of night vision binoculars.

"I think this is our guy," she announced, keeping her eyes on the biker as he mounted a black motorcycle only slightly different from all the others. "With any luck, he'll take us to Dayna."

For once, Grayson didn't try to argue. "We'll pick you up just beyond the gate."

The lone biker's motorcycle roared as it exited the property on the road ahead of her. As Bexley approached the guard, she slipped her phone back into her pocket and feigned intoxication. "M' ride's here," she slurred to the man, pointing at the deputy's undercover cruiser.

The man tipped an imaginary hat. "Have a good evening, sweetheart."

She wobbled toward the car and jumped into the backseat. "Don't lose him," she told Danks, patting the driver's seat.

"Not a chance," he replied, shifting into drive and pushing on the accelerator.

Grayson hadn't said much to Bexley since their clipped conversation outside the salon, and she was unnerved by the silent treatment he projected from the passenger's seat as Danks tailed the sleek black Harley Davidson from a safe distance. The biker headed onto the interstate toward L.A., his taillights weaving in and out of traffic until exiting on the south side several miles later.

Bexley laughed when the motorcycle slowed outside Big Dick's Inn. "What is it about this place that draws unsavory characters? Vibrating beds?"

Grayson turned to her, eyebrows lowered. "You've been here?"

The biker removed his helmet as he approached one of the motel room doors, passkey in hand. From across the street, Bexley was only able to see a shock of his honey wheat colored hair and his thick brown beard. He slipped inside the room without incident. The curtains were tightly drawn.

"Not much else we can do at this point," Danks said. "Either we wait it out to see if he's in there alone, or I give you a ride back."

"I'm not going anywhere until we find out," Bexley answered.

As time ticked by, she bounced around on the backseat with unbridled energy. She sent Kiersten and Cineste several texts, letting them know they'd either reached a dead end or they were on the cusp of finding the alleged victim.

It wasn't long before Danks sat taller behind the driver's seat. "Someone's coming out."

Right as Bexley looked up, a slender woman with dirty blond hair closed the motel room door while puffing on a vape pen. She wore a tank top and shorts along with a baseball cap, its brim low over her eyes. But Bexley had no qualms about the girl's identity.

Dayna Stryker was alive, and appeared unharmed.

Better yet, there was something around her neck that sparkled beneath the motel's lights like a million dollars worth of diamonds.

CHAPTER NINETEEN

The motel phone rang for several minutes without an answer. Finally, a snappy, *"What do you want?"*

Excitement rippled through Bexley's limbs. "Good evenin', this is Doris from management," she said with a slight southern twang. "One of our guests reported a water leak in their ceilin', and we discovered a burst pipe on the second floor. Would you mind if we stopped by to check on y'all's room?"

"Our room is *fine*," the young woman Bexley suspected to be Dayna snarled. "No water on the ceiling."

"It'll only take a minute, then we'll be out of your hair. I know it's an inconvenience, but we need to make sure our ceiling isn't going to fall in or our insurance agent will be up our ass. We'll throw in a free drink to the bar next-door for your trouble."

Dayna let out a dramatic sigh. There was a brief noise like she had covered the phone with her hand, followed by a short, muffled conversation. Then, "Okay, fine. Whatever."

Bexley tossed the burner phone back into her handbag, then grinned at Deputy Danks. "I'm in."

Grayson rubbed at his furrowed forehead. "I'm not convinced this is the best way to go. The judge could find you in contempt for becoming involved if that's really the alleged victim in there. And that biker could be packing."

"The two of you will only be a block away," Bexley scolded. "If I sense any trouble, I'll be out of there faster than you can say bail jumper."

"Is that supposed to make me feel better?" he growled, folding his arms with a piercing glare.

"We'll keep a close eye on the situation," Danks promised. He pulled down on the edge of Bexley's shirt, double-checking that the wire was in place. "You should be good to go. Just remember, you have to stay within ten feet of her, or the mic won't pick up everything she's saying."

Bexley nodded. "Keep it cozy—got it."

"And don't go saying anything smart that'll make her angry," Grayson called after her just as she was closing the car door. With a sigh, she realized he was only getting worse. She was to the point where she would say something unforgivable.

As she walked the short block in the chilling darkness, she was certain it would stretch on forever. It felt as if someone was watching her every step of the way. Paranoia pressed heavily onto her shoulders. The people who set her up had confiscated her gun. Just how far were they willing to go to make her look guilty?

Breath held, she knocked on the outside door where she'd seen the biker and Dayna. "Good evening! It's Doris from the front office. I'm here with someone from maintenance."

"Hold on!" a female voice panted.

A solid minute ticked by before Dayna answered the door. Blond hair ruffled and flipped to one side, cheeks pinched with pink, it would seem that Bexley had caught them mid-coitus. Aside from the collar, Dayna only wore an oversized white t-shirt that barely covered her lean, tanned thighs. When her arm reached out to brace the doorway, Bexley couldn't help but notice white gauze covered both of the girl's forearms from wrist to elbow. *Someone had a peculiar boo-boo,* Bexley mused.

Behind the girl, a man with several years on Dayna lounged on the unmade bed in worn blue jeans, picking the cellophane off a pack of cigarettes. Bexley tried not to gawk, but his build was toned and sculpted, complete with an impressive Adonis Belt. Tattoos of all colors, shapes, and sizes adorned his body, some even covering the back of his hands. The unruliness of his brown hair worn long on the top, shaved on the sides, made it appear he'd been finger-combing it for hours. A well-groomed mustache and beard that perfectly matched the color of his thick eyebrows gave his strong facial contours a hard edge, completing the bad boy look.

As she watched him, Bexley's pulse throbbed in her throat. He had to be the biker she followed from the clubhouse. Despite being incredibly attractive, he gave the impression of being an insane amount of trouble. He could also be dangerous, and she was unarmed. She hoped Alex and Grayson were keeping a close eye on her every move as promised.

"You *work* here?" Dayna snapped with a cold laugh, eyes dragging up and down Bexley's tank top and short skirt. "I'm guessing you charge an hourly rate?"

"Are you saying you don't recognize this face?" Bexley deadpanned, pointing at herself with one hand and removing the wig with the other. "Would it help if I were drugged and tied to a chair?" A burst of anger tightened her expression. "You set me up, *Dayna.*"

Dayna stepped back, preparing to shut the door in her face. "Sorry. I have no idea what you're talking about."

Bexley dropped the wig and snatched the girl's elbow, lifting her bandaged wrist between them. "Looks like you lost a little blood. Perhaps just enough to taint a knife and paint the inside of your vehicle to look like a serious crime scene? And that's an awfully expensive *necklace.* Where'd you get it? Pet Expo?"

"Bexley?" a low voice asked behind her, the man's tone unreadable. Bexley jolted, wondering how she managed to get on the biker's radar. "Is that really you?"

Fingering the collar, Dayna turned to look at him, giving Bexley an unobstructed view of the man. "You *know* her?"

"Hell yeah." The man tapped a cigarette

against the pack as his warm brown eyes dragged over Bexley's costume. He chuckled. "We went to high school together."

Bexley tilted her head, wondering how she could've possibly forgotten anyone so utterly unforgettable. "I'm sorry, but I don't—"

"Brewer Hawkins." Sticking a cigarette between his lips, his mouth tilted with an adorable smirk—deep dimples included. "I used to cheat off you in Anatomy."

A flicker of recollection came to the surface. Was he seriously the scrawny loner she always caught staring over her shoulder in class? Part of her always let him by with it, because between the way he dressed in tattered clothing and kept to himself, she assumed the poor kid came from a rough home. "How unfortunate for you. I barely passed that class."

His full lips spread into a toothy smile. "So I found out."

"This little reunion is great and everything," Dayna seethed, threatening to shut the door, "but I'd really like it if you'd leave now."

"What are you going to do? Call the cops?" Bexley waved an arm through the air. "*Please* do! I'll even dial them *for* you! They've been searching everywhere for you, Dayna, so much that they've assumed—thanks to the bogus clues you left behind —that you're dead. I'm being charged with your *murder*. I'd be more than happy to inform them that you're alive and well. They'd also be interested in hearing how you came into possession of stolen property."

"Wait a minute." Brewer dropped the pack of cigarettes and bolted to his feet. In two steps, he was clutching Dayna's arm. "What'd you do? Why the hell would they think Bexley killed you?"

Dayna scowled, struggling to get away. "What do you care?"

"Because she's one of the last *good* ones!" he roared, his face becoming a deep scarlet.

"The bitch had our daddy sent to prison!" Dayna disagreed with a violent shake of her head. "His career is ruined because of her! No one will ever hire him again!"

Brewer's nostrils flared. "Doesn't make what you did to her right. Your *daddy* should've gone to prison for a lot more than solicitation, sweetheart."

Tears splashed against Dayna's cheeks. "I did it so we could be together, baby! Daddy will never let me be with you! This was the only way!"

"Sweetheart," he said with a chuckle, "this ain't

a fairytale. There's no happily ever after with a guy like me. If you want a Prince Charming, you should hook up with one of those rich pricks your daddy wants you to date. I have enough problems on my own without worrying how I'm going to support your spoiled ass. We had fun, but this was never going to be anything substantial." Thick brows lowered, he gestured in Bexley's direction. "What the hell did you think you were going to accomplish by sending her to jail? Didn't you think they would eventually figure out what had really happened— that you're alive and well?"

"It was all *Ali's* fault!" Dayna wailed. "She got the Mayor and Maci's dad involved, and they said they knew a full-proof way to send her away! Ali gave me the collar she stole from that lady as payment! She said I could live a posh life if I sold it!"

Bexley pulled the wire out from inside her shirt, and held it out for Dayna to see. "Can you say that a little louder for the folks in the back?"

Dayna paled, shuffling back against Brewer. "The cops sent you?"

"Even one better," Bexley answered with a wink. "There's a sheriff's deputy and a police detective monitoring our conversation from just down the street. If you listen carefully, you'll hear the poetic sounds of a siren any second now."

A heartbeat later, the wail of Deputy Danks's siren cut through the darkness. Relief washed over Bexley's shoulders. The nightmare was over. For her, anyway. Grayson would still have to delve into an investigation involving Kappa Kappa Delta's rushing techniques, and both Kayla and Violet would have to testify. She was just grateful to know the life-altering charges would no longer be looming over her head.

Dayna spun around, grabbing onto Brewer. "Babe, you have to get me out of here! I can't go to jail! I wouldn't even last an hour in a place like that!"

Brewer removed her hands from his shoulders. "Sounds like your problem, *babe*." He backed away, stuffing his hands into his jeans and shrugging. "I want nothing to do with this. I never would've agreed to meet you here tonight if I had known the whole story. Hell, I would've turned you in myself if I'd known the truth. I'm not going to jail for anyone."

Deputy Danks's car parked in the lot behind

them, its siren giving one final warning blurt. Dayna went into a wild rage, screaming and swinging her arms at Brewer. *"You asshole! I did this to be with you! I thought you loved me!"*

Danks stepped in and pulled her off, reciting the Miranda rights as he half-carried her back to the squad car. Bexley and Brewer trailed after them, stopping just outside the room on the sidewalk.

Bexley turned to Brewer. "You alright?"

"This is nothing new. I tend to bring out the best in women like her." He retrieved another cigarette from his back pocket, and lit it with a Zippo. Smoke billowed from his nose when he smirked back in Bexley's direction. "What about you? Beating a murder rap must feel pretty damn good. You're turning into a real outlaw."

A nervous laugh fell from Bexley's lips. "You have no idea."

Grayson suddenly appeared, stepping in beside her. "You're lucky that went down in your favor. Things could've gotten ugly, Bex. What if she'd been carrying a weapon?" He curled an arm around her shoulders while giving Brewer a hard, accusatory look. "You look familiar. Who're you again?"

Brewer grunted. "Don't matter." His eyes cut down to the badge and gun holster on Grayson's belt. "We weren't friends back in the day, and we sure as hell aren't friends now."

A tick passed over Grayson's jaw. "They're going to want you to come down to the Sheriff's station for questioning."

"And why's that?" Brewer challenged, blowing a puff of smoke in Grayson's direction. "Whatever that crazy girl got involved in has nothin' to do with me."

"That's for the sheriff to decide," Grayson snarled, moving his head to avoid the tail end of the smoke billowing from Brewer's cigarette. "We can do this one of two ways. You can willingly come in *now* on your own, or they'll issue a warrant for your punk ass. You look as if you know how that kind of thing works."

Holding Grayson's glare, Brewer blew another stream from his nostrils. "Matter of fact, I don't." He flicked the lit cigarette to the ground. "My *punk ass* hasn't had so much as a parking ticket."

Bexley twisted away from Grayson to step between them. Chances seemed favorable that the biker was no longer anything like the nice kid she'd once known, but he'd stood up for her against Dayna. Least she could do was return the favor. "I've seen enough WrestleMania to know how this ends." She spread her fingertips across Brewer's chest, regretting her actions when she sensed Grayson's entire body tensing even more. "You're going to drive yourself to the sheriff's station, right?"

Brewer stared Grayson down for a moment longer, then glanced Bexley's way and nodded. "Yeah. I got nothin' to hide."

Bexley withdrew her hand and turned to face Grayson. "See, there's nothing to worry about. Why don't you call Kiersten and the others to let them know it's over? I'm sure they're waiting with baited breath to hear how this ended."

Grayson threw Brewer one last pointed look before he stomped off with his phone pressed to his ear. Bexley didn't want to consider all the negative things he'd likely have to say about Brewer once they were alone.

Brewer was quiet for a beat, watching Bexley closely. There was a sudden intensity behind his gaze that made her feel unsettled. "You with that guy?"

"Days like this, I'm not so sure." Smiling, she

laughed and rolled her eyes. "The details of our relationship are complicated…best left for another conversation. But I'm really sorry he treated you like a criminal. He had no right."

"No worries. I stereotyped him right back as an overbearing prick who wouldn't know a good time if it bit him in the ass. Seems that's the way I remembered him being in high school, too." With a grin, he lifted one shoulder. "Got an invite to the upcoming ten year class reunion. You goin'?"

"Pretty sure my reputation as a ball-buster voided my invite." That, and she had recently learned Grayson's ex was in charge of the event. "What about you?"

"One of the reasons I became a Coastie was to get away from those pricks. Guessing by your boyfriend's reaction, I wouldn't be too welcome anyway."

"Grayson's not usually like that." *Was he?* Or had she been too involved in their budding relationship to notice he resembled the elite residents of Papaya Springs? Shaking the thought, Bexley squinted at Brewer. "Sorry if this makes me sound like one of them, but I don't remember seeing you at graduation."

"Considerin' you were one of few classmates

who never picked on me, you could *never* sound like one of them," he scolded with a fierce look. "And since I got the invite, you're not the only one who forgot I enlisted early senior year…got my GED a few months later. Couldn't wait to get the hell away from home."

Empathy spread through her chest. "I know the feeling."

His gaze slowly assessed the features of her face before his lips spread with a smile. "You look great, by the way. *Real* good. Haven't changed a bit."

She shifted her stance, wishing he'd look away. "Me? Look at you! What exactly did they feed you in the military? I don't see a single trace of the skinny kid who was too shy to speak up in class. Did you eat him? Should I be concerned that he's in there somewhere, trying to bust out?"

Brushing his toes over something on the sidewalk, he chuckled quietly. "That kid went through a lot before he became a man. Best left for another conversation." Turning back toward the motel room, he slipped another unlit cigarette between his lips. "Bein' you know where I live now and everything, maybe we can meet up some time. For drinks, or…whatever."

"You live here?" Her eyebrows shot upward as she studied the shabby building. "In this motel?"

"It's temporary…'til I figure things out. You know?" Shrugging, he lit the cigarette and inhaled deeply before his lips quirked with a charming smile. "Don't be a stranger, Bexley."

CHAPTER TWENTY

Bexley and Grayson returned to Luke's firm the following morning, accompanied by Temperance Rose. She'd first been relieved when Bexley called to fill her in on everything that had happened, then she broke down in tears after hearing the details of Kayla's betrayal. But the former reality star looked more like herself as she waited inside the leather and mahogany infused conference room at Bexley's side, hair and makeup done up to camera-ready standards.

Kayla appeared in the doorway before long. She froze in place with the site of Temperance, nearly causing her parents to bowl her over from behind. "What's this?" she demanded. "No one told me *she'd* be here."

Luke rose behind the head of the colossal table, palms of his hands held out. Despite not wearing one of his usual designer suits, he still commanded the room in a crisp white button down rolled at the sleeves, dark hair neatly combed. "Miss Rose requested this meeting so she can work out a deal with you, Miss Dahl. One that wouldn't involve the police."

Kayla's father, a tall and intimidating-looking man in his fifties, closed the door behind them and gently nudged Kayla forward. "Let's hear what they have to say." It seemed as if everyone in the room was collectively holding their breaths until the family of three sat across from Bexley and Temperance.

"Before we begin," Luke said, holding Kayla's perplexed expression, "I want to acknowledge that I represent Miss Rose, and therefore cannot give you any advice on your legal course of action. You're encouraged to retain your own attorney before you make any decisions."

Kayla collapsed against the plush leather chair, appearing even more exhausted than Bexley felt. The girl's normally luxurious hair hung limp around her head like it had enough shenanigans. Her fingers turned white as she gripped the arms of the chair, and addressed Temperance. "I don't know what they did with the collar. I swear. I'm so sorry. I just want this to be over."

Her father threw Kayla a scolding glance. Bexley noted that he was especially fit, and figured it must've been from the hard labor required of farming. He pointed a dark, cracked index finger at his daughter. "You never should've taken that dog off the property in the first place."

"Bexley found the collar," Temperance told her in an even, unaffected tone. "Consider yourself *afortunado*."

"For real?" Kayla squeaked, eyes wide.

Luke lowered back down to his chair, nodding. "It's in police custody as we speak."

"Praise Jesus," the mom whispered, dropping her tense shoulders.

Luke passed a stapled document to the woman. "Miss Rose is offering Kayla immunity to all charges under the condition that she'll testify against Alicia Stryker and the other members of Kappa Kappa Delta who were involved in both Miss Squires's kidnapping, *and* the incident that put Violet Baker in a coma."

"I'll do it," Kayla blurted, wiping at her wet face. "I'm so sorry, Temperance—about everything!

You know I would *never* hurt Cinderella, and it was never my intention to steal from you. I should've come forward sooner. I should've told someone what was going on there. Maybe I could've stopped them before they…they almost *killed* one of my best friends!" The girl burst into sobs, burying her face in her mother's bosom.

Kayla's mother, a small and meek woman with slight crows feet, dragged her distraught daughter in close against her side. "It was never her intention to hurt you, Temperance. She thought they were asking her to perform a harmless prank. It's my fault she felt pressured to become a Delta."

Bexley's lips twitched with irritation. "My idea of a *harmless prank* would involve tinfoil or toilet paper, and not luring a woman into being kidnapped and set up for fabricated murder charges."

"They made me call you!" Kayla insisted among sobs, vehemently shaking her head. *"I didn't want to do it, I swear!"*

Luke stood, clearing his throat as he addressed the Dahls. "Why don't you take a moment to review the agreement with Kayla in private? I'll have my secretary escort you to my office."

As Luke paged his secretary, the family rose

together, supporting Kayla. On their way to the door, the mother paused, eyeing Temperance over her shoulder. "Thank you for your kindness, Miss Rose. Kayla's a good girl…she just made a really poor choice. I hope you find it in your heart to forgive her."

Temperance's expression hardened. "Perhaps one day—once she fully realizes the consequences of her actions."

The family had nothing more to say as the father once again closed the door behind them.

Temperance rose before reaching down to squeeze Bexley's hand. *"Gracias*, Miss Bexley. Being betrayed by someone I trusted wasn't the outcome I was hoping for, but perhaps I will sleep better now that *Cenicienta's* precious collar has been found."

Bexley nodded, rising alongside her. "I hope you're able to find some kind of peace, and move on."

"I'll be in touch once they've signed the agreement," Luke told her.

Temperance nodded in acknowledgement, flashing a sincere smile. Bexley was certain she could already see a change in the woman's attitude since their last meeting as Temperance exited the room.

Grayson turned to Luke once they were alone. "What's the status of Bexley's situation?"

The attorney's lips twisted into a confident smile. "The assistant district attorney already filed a dismissal of all charges with the court. Needless to say, ADA Holmes was rather bitter about the whole thing. She was practically snarling when she came into my office to personally serve the papers."

Relief washed over Bexley. She paused to swallow the lump of relief clogging her throat. "Guess I'll have to change that appointment for a prison tat into 'I heart ADA Holmes'."

Luke chuckled. "Right. Since you're still out on bond, the judge has set a hearing for three o'clock this afternoon."

"What will happen to Dayna and Alicia Stryker?" Grayson asked. "The DA? The *Mayor?*"

"It's too early to say." Luke reclined in his chair with a thoughtful look. "After Ms. Stryker was brought in, the sheriff's office started conducting interviews with all those allegedly involved. Since Lieutenant Baker demanded they have a special prosecutor brought in to handle their cases, the process could be drawn out longer than usual."

"They're going to deny everything," Bexley grumbled, lacing her fingers inside her newly cut hair. "It's the word of a twenty-year-old against some of the most powerful men in the city—ones who are known for being tight with the sheriff, I might add." Though her memories from that night were still cloudy, Bexley had a strong hunch the two men had an active role in her kidnapping. "This town will never know true justice as long as money talks."

Luke gave her a defeated look. "I know it's frustrating, but there's not a lot we can do right now other than cross our fingers that they'll at least be brought up on charges. I'll keep you updated on the situation as best as I can." He stood, offering to shake Bexley's hand. "In the meantime, try to stay out of trouble. At least until this afternoon's hearing."

Bexley shook his hand and shrugged. "You're asking an awful lot of me. This *is* Papaya Springs."

Grayson shook the attorney's hand next. "Thanks, Luke. I appreciate all you've done."

"I'm always willing to do whatever it takes to stop this city from being taken over by corruption." Luke release Grayson's hand, and tipped his head at Bexley. "Can I ask *you* a favor?"

"Not if it involves making more enemies. I've made enough to last several lifetimes."

"Does that mean you're ready to give up the PI gig?" Grayson asked, his eyes suddenly lit with hope.

Something dark stirred through Bexley. In that moment, she all at once knew she was done entertaining his fears. "Just as soon as you quit being a detective."

Luke cleared his throat. "Uh, it's nothing like that." Pink spread through his cheeks when he gave her a timid smile. "I was wondering if you could help me out in choosing Kiersten's favorite flower."

A small ripple of jealousy bubbled in Bexley's chest. She'd give anything to remove the complications from her relationship with Grayson. With a hearty laugh, she patted Luke's shoulder. "Buddy, I don't have a clue. But I guarantee you'll win her over with a good bottle of Prosecco."

NEITHER GRAYSON nor Bexley spoke as he drove out of the firm's parking lot. Bexley sensed he was as reluctant as she felt to discuss anything involving their relationship. They had yet to address everything that happened before she was arrested.

"This has been one crazy week," she started,

peering over at him. "Too bad we didn't get to take that vacation, am I right?"

His lips tightened. "My mom told me about the conversation you had the other night. She was pretty upset."

Bexley's shoulders dropped forward. "Sorry, but I was sitting outside the sorority, getting ready to confront them about Violet when she called. She was getting real pushy…started mentioning babies…and *marriage*. I guess I kind of lost it."

"Do you want any of that?" His eyes didn't stray from the road, as if he was afraid he'd see the wrong answer written all over her face. He knew her too well. "Children? Marriage?"

"Some day, sure. I mean…*maybe*." Her heart thudded painfully. "The circumstances would have to be different. We can't raise a child under these conditions. Look what happened to your lieutenant's daughter."

"What happened to Violet was completely unrelated to his position."

"Still. You said he doesn't let anyone know he has a daughter for that very reason. Besides, I don't have room to worry about diapers and PTA when I'm dodging kidnappers and murder conspiracies."

"So quit…go back into journalism." He turned

to her and lifted an eyebrow with a little smile tugging at his lips. "Better yet, you could always take some time off to raise kids."

The temptation to slam her head into the dashboard was overwhelming. "I actually *enjoy* what I do. Why is it so hard for you to accept the fact that I want to be involved in the same line of work as you? Is it because I'm a woman?"

He appeared ready to fire back when his phone rang over the speakers. The thick tension between them instantly lifted the second he accepted the call. "Detective Rivers."

"Hey, Rivers!" a rolling voice responded. "It's Al from Hawkins Auto Body! Do you know a way I can get in touch with Bexley? I left several messages a couple days ago letting her know that her vehicle's been patched up, but she hasn't stopped by or returned my call."

Bexley's stomach dropped. The state of her vehicle was not a conversation she wanted Grayson involved in under any circumstances. "Hey, Al!" she called out. "You can just leave it outside with the keys in the visor—we'll pick it up in a little while— okay thanks—bye!"

Grayson eyed her quizzically. The words had come out faster than intended, but she was desperate to end the call. There couldn't be a worse time for the truth to come to light.

To her horror, Al continued to ramble. "You're a lucky bastard, Rivers. Any woman who can dodge bullets like a gangster must be a hellfire—"

Bexley stabbed at the end call button on the car's control center, heart lurching.

"What's going on?" Grayson demanded, clutching the steering wheel. "Why does Al think you can 'dodge bullets'?"

Covering her arm over her eyes, Bexley took a deep, calming breath. Their relationship had already taken a hard left. Lying to him would be pointless. "The night I agreed to take Temperance's case, I stopped by the condo to change before heading to your place." She peered over at him. "Someone shot at me in the parking lot."

Grayson calmly steered the Bronco to the side of the road, and shifted into park. He sat tall, scowling at the quiet residential road ahead. "You must not've called the police, or I would've heard about it long before now. Did you at least get a good look at the shooter?"

"No."

Draping his arms over the steering wheel, he rested his head on top. "You always say my job is just as dangerous as yours. But at least I tell you everything that goes on with mine. I don't hide things from you."

She knew they had reached a point of no return, and she didn't know how to fix it. Telling him she would change would be an outright lie. "I knew you'd get angry." Looking away, she sighed. "What do you want me to say?"

He sat upright again and shifted back into first before making a wide U-Turn.

Bexley's mouth dried. Was he taking her to the station to report the shooting? "Where are you going?"

"I'm taking you to get your car." When he glanced over at her, his expression was as cold as she'd ever seen. "I think you should stay at your place for awhile."

CHAPTER TWENTY-ONE

Back at the condo she shared with her sister, Bexley curled her hair and applied a touch of makeup while wavering on her feet. The sordid events of the last several days had been exhausting. Sorting through her issues with Grayson had almost been as emotionally draining as being accused of murder. More than anything, she wanted to sleep for days.

She wandered into her closet, belatedly remembering the bulk of her wardrobe had migrated to Grayson's. With any luck, she could retrieve her belongings while he was at work so they wouldn't have to beat the proverbial dead horse yet again.

Even though their tastes couldn't be any different, she headed into Cineste's room to rifle through her closet. She was only in there a moment before soft footsteps fell behind her. "I'm sorry, do you think you live here or something?"

Snorting, Bexley shoved aside a cluster of hangers. "Do you own anything that *isn't* pink or frilly?"

"Don't be a jerk to my clothes!" Cineste stepped between Bexley and the closet with her hands on her hips. "What are you doing here, anyway? Why are you in my closet?"

"Grayson took me to get my car from the repair shop. It was closer to swing by here than to drive all the way back to his place, and I need to look presentable when the judge declares me a free woman."

"I'm so happy this mess is finally over." Cineste turned to thumb through her selection of dresses. "Now I can ask you something without worrying you have too much going on and can't handle it." She plucked a flowing red jumpsuit off the rod, and shoved it into Bexley's arms. "Try this."

"If you're going to ask me to make animal balloons in this thing, the answer's a hard no."

"Always the joker." With a toothy smile, Cineste grasped her sister's shoulders. "You probably didn't even notice that all of Alex's things have been here for weeks now. He's officially moved in…gave up his lease. We're hoping you'd also make *your* move into Grayson's place official so we can take over your bigger room and make mine into a home gym. Do you mind?"

A whoosh of disappointment swept through Bexley. She was being evicted from her own home. Despite having nowhere else to go, Bexley didn't have the heart to crush her sister's plans. She forced a convincing smile. "Of course not. I'll have the rest of my things out by tomorrow."

Cineste jumped up and down, giggling like the pigtailed little girl who once looked up at her big sister like she was her biggest hero. "Oh my god, Bex, I think Alex is The One! He's being so sweet about everything! He keeps talking about our future, and what it would be like if we had kids!" Then she flung her arms around her sister. "We're so in love! I get the feeling it won't be long until he'll ask me to marry him!"

A sincere smile slipped over Bexley's lips. "I'm happy for you, Cin. I really am. Alex seems like a good man." *One I should've listened to from the beginning.*

Half an hour before her hearing, Bexley sensed with a mere glance across the parking lot that something about her Expedition was amiss. Once closer, she discovered all four of the tires were completely flat. *Slashed.*

"Oh, come on." Feeling something deep inside herself breaking, she dropped her handbag onto the pavement. Her meter for bullshit had reached full capacity.

Behind where she stood in the middle of the parking lot, the deep rumble of a motorcycle approached. *Go ahead, run me over,* she thought, closing her eyes. *End the misery.*

The motorcycle's engine was cut. Then there was a low chuckle from right behind her. "You really can't catch a break lately, huh?"

She spun around on her sensible flats to find Brewer perched on his black motorcycle in full leather riding gear, helmet resting in his lap. For some reason, knowing he had come there to seek her out for whatever reason brought a sudden rush of tears to her eyes. Blinking the moisture back, she snorted. "What can I say…my fan club continues to grow by leaps and bounds."

His white teeth sparkled in the afternoon

sunlight when he smiled. "Can I give you a lift somewhere?"

She eyed the black monstrosity wearily. She hadn't been on the back of a motorcycle since she'd gone with a friend in college. The experience of speeding down the streets of Manhattan on a foreign crotch rocket had been downright terrifying. "You're kidding, right?"

He held the helmet out to her, chuckling. His black leather jacket featuring his club's logo creaked with every movement. "If you're worried about flashing me in that dress, I promise I'll shut my eyes when you climb on."

She wasn't the girly type by any stretch of the imagination, but she had put in more effort than usual to appear presentable. And she had gone with her sister's most modest choices of dresses that extended down to her ankles. Still, it was vital that she arrive on time to her hearing. "What are you doing here, anyway?"

"Thought I'd check in, see how you were coping after everything that went down."

Suspicion rang through her head. "Is my address etched into some bathroom stall?"

He answered with a sheepish smile. "Saw it on your ticket at the repair shop."

Tilting her head, she balked. "I had no idea you worked there."

"I actually own the place." He lifted both shoulders matter-of-fact like. "Started it up right after I got out of the military."

Her eyes rounded. *Hawkins Auto Body*. It never occurred to her that the auto body shop would have a connection to her long-lost classmate. "I pictured you more as the white collar type—like a Wall Street broker, or maybe an English professor."

"Never cared much for Shakespeare." His deep dimples flared as he wiggled the helmet between them. "Come on. What are you afraid of? A little wind in your hair? I promise it'll only make that hairdo even sexier."

In that moment, Bexley realized how refreshing it felt to be encouraged to do something dangerous. When was the last time she'd hung out with a man who wasn't trying to control her every move? She always enjoyed spending time with Kiersten, but they didn't have a lot of interests in common. Befriending someone who embraced her wild side could be entertaining. She was ready to literally let her hair down, and enjoy herself.

She stepped toward him, unprepared when he hooked her around the waist and tugged her closer.

She let out a squeak and caught herself against his sturdy shoulders. Bottom lip held between his teeth, he slipped the helmet over her head and tightened the strap beneath her chin. She watched up close as golden speckles in his eyes reflected the sunlight beneath dark, thick lashes. *How many girls had fallen under their spell?*

When finished, he gestured over his shoulder and grinned. "Hop on, kiddo. Careful your leg doesn't bump the muffler on the other side."

She gathered the bottom half of the skirt in one hand, and climbed onto the buttery soft seat behind him. The rich scent of man and leather warmed her belly as she wrapped her arms around his waist.

He braced his feet on the pavement on either side. "Where we headin'?"

"The courthouse...time to collect my ticket to freedom."

The engine roared beneath them, vibrating through every inch of Bexley's body. She squeezed her arms a little tighter around Brewer's lean build, a little afraid she'd fall off. But the ride itself was incredibly freeing. She couldn't remember the last time she felt so alive.

Inside the courtroom, Luke waited for Bexley at the defendant's table, and Brewer sat behind them. Otherwise, the gallery was empty. Bexley couldn't help feeling a sense of abandonment despite knowing everyone had their reasons for not being there. Besides, they all knew the charges were being dismissed. Still, their lack of interest in seeing her released stung a little.

The hearing itself was short and sweet. After the dismissal was entered into record by Assistant District Attorney Holmes, the judge ordered Bexley's bail be exonerated. Then it was over.

After the ADA collected her file and turned to leave the courtroom, she paused to throw Bexley what could only be described as a warning glare.

"Call me," Bexley said, miming a phone with her hand. "We can meet up for drinks."

Luke chuckled as the woman stomped away. "Congratulations," he told Bexley, shaking her hand. "You're officially free to go about your life. Can I offer you a ride somewhere?"

Bexley eyed Brewer as he leaned back against the court bench, arms and ankles crossed, smirk pressed to his lips. "Thanks, but I already have a ride."

Luke followed her gaze and frowned. "Right."

It was on the tip of Bexley's tongue to call him out for being judgmental, but Brewer lifted his chin to Luke in greeting, and Luke nodded back. Maybe Grayson's reaction to Brewer had made her paranoid.

Turning back to her, Luke cleared his throat. "Let me know if I can be of service in the future. It was a pleasure representing you, Bexley."

"Thanks for everything. I get the feeling I'll be seeing more of you…only not in the courtroom." She added a cheesy wink, and Luke laughed in good-nature.

She took her time trailing out behind him, even though she all at once felt giddy and had the strange urge to jump into Brewer's arms.

"So what do you feel like doing now?"

"I'm not sure." She was free to do…anything she wanted, if only she knew what it was.

"It's a nice day for a cruise down to the beach."

The exhaustion she'd felt before court all at once evaporated. It was the perfect time to take off, and collect her thoughts. She grinned back at him from ear-to-ear. "I could use a little fresh air."

"Then lets get the hell outta here," Brewer said, tilting his head toward the exit.

They walked out of the courthouse side-by-side,

neither of them saying a word until they were met by a young redhead in handcuffs being escorted by a sheriff's deputy. She wore a barely-there jeans skirt and a low-cut top that made Bexley wonder if the girl had been arrested for soliciting.

"Hey, Brewer," the redhead purred. "Where've you been, handsome? I've missed you."

Brewer stuffed a hand in his jeans pocket and turned, walking backwards while flashing the girl a big smile. "Around."

The girl's green eyes stayed on Brewer as the deputy led her away. "Wanna party later?"

"Looks like you're a little busy, sweetheart," he answered, chuckling. "Maybe another time."

"Call me!" the girl called over her shoulder.

Bexley snorted under her breath as they continued toward the parking lot. "You should consider moonlighting at a daycare. You seem to have a way with young women."

He shrugged. "Can't help it that they find me attractive."

"It must be difficult to be so popular."

Just then, they spotted ADA Holmes engaged in a heated argument with DA Jenkins behind a black sedan. The two spotted Bexley and froze, throwing her matching looks of disgust.

Brewer laughed rather heartily. "Seems you've established a popularity of your own."

Once they reached his motorcycle, he again fastened the helmet straps beneath her chin before she climbed onto the motorcycle behind him.

"Are you hungry?" he asked. "I know this place. It serves the best ribs. It's called—"

"—Rib King," Bexley finished. "Isn't that the place that got raided by the health department?"

"Haven't gotten sick yet," Brewer said, glancing over his shoulder with a smile. "And I eat there all the time."

Bexley couldn't even imagine Grayson indulging in questionable ribs. "Do they serve beer?"

"Their liquor license got revoked, but I have a flask of whiskey in my saddle bag." She could feel his chest rumble with laughter. "Take a walk on the wild side, Bexley."

As the engine roared to life beneath them, Bexley decided she was going to take his suggestion to heart.

Dear Reader,

Thank you for following Bexley's adventures so far! Please take a minute to leave a review on Goodreads and Amazon or the website from which you purchased your copy. Reviews don't have to be long or perfect. Even one sentence can help to spread the word!

As always, I appreciate your support!

ABOUT THE AUTHOR

With over 40 captivating titles spanning various genres, Quinn Avery honed her talent for crafting intricate puzzles through her smart and quirky Bexley Squires mystery series. Her contemporary suspense thrillers, often set in her beloved locales such as Lake Shetek and Mankato, Minnesota, are nothing short of addictive, leaving readers spellbound with their mind-spinning twists.

For more information, and a free ebook, visit www.QuinnAvery.com.

ACKNOWLEDGMENTS

To Najla Qamber: Thank you for humoring me by creating another stunning cover with my daughter's image! I'm tickled with the finished product!

To Jenny Hanson: Thanks again for loaning me your eagle eyes, and for being a loyal fan!

To my editor, Jodi Henley: you rock, lady! I'm having a blast creating this series with you, and look forward to our next project!

To Corrie Hanson: Thanks for always having my back, no matter the situation! You've been an amazing friend throughout my journey!

To Shawna Barnett, Lisa Frommie, and Josh Frommie: Thanks for your patience and expertise!

To my super librarian friend, Heidi Schutt: Thank you for supporting my journey, and providing valuable feedback! Bago is lucky to have you!

To the local businesses/libraries and bloggers who have helped to promote my work: I'm thankful beyond words!

To my writer friends (notably Tracy, Micki, Kristie, Sierra, Leesa, Diana, Pam, Mira, Aubrey): Thank for you always being there. I love you all to pieces, and thank my lucky stars for having such talented friends!

To my "regular" friends who are anything BUT regular, and who have supported my career over the years (notably April, Denise, Michelle, Tara, Lori, Amy, Laura, Janet, Jess, Teresa, Misty, Krista, Cindy, Carolyn, and "crazy" Michelle): I wish I could buy you all a fabulous vacation for putting up with me, and being there at my signings! I have so much love for you all! 🤍

To my mom and dad: Thanks for being so supportive of my career!

To my husband and children: Thanks for always being there, and putting up with my crap. 🤍 And SJ, you should be modeling. Just sayin'.

To my fans, new and old: THANK YOU from the bottom of my heart for giving my new heroine a chance! I hope you've enjoyed the series so far!

9 7 9 8 9 8 9 5 5 5 2 5 3